THREADING

OF THE SOUL

THREADING

OF THE SOUL

ReMembering Oneness
and the Multidimensional Self

BEKI CROWELL

Book jacket design: Tamra Scott
Book interior design: Kai Evans
Editor credits: Shanen Johnson
Photo credit: Banner Adams

Artwork created by Beki
The front cover of this book
is the Soul Portrait of Shahalaku
The back cover is a
painting representing the frequency of the
Soul Language, Weeshah'aneylo,
along with the portrait of Beki created by Elayna Shakur

Published 2024
in the United States of America

ISBN: 978-1-7326566-1-1

SOUL ART

To my beloved

Little did I know when I began this creation
that this would become a love story.
Your Love inspires me, grounds me,
and "quenches my fire!"

Contents

Dear Reader

This story is a Divine transmission from the Soul Self — from mine and the collective Soul with which we are all One. Therefore, the typical literary rules do not always apply here, requiring creative ways to express the message and frequency delivered within the story. You may notice that certain words are capitalized, such as Wholeness and Creation, Awakening, Sacred Breath, and Beauty. Capitalizing them adds emphasis, importance, sacredness, and a higher frequency, connoting a Divine quality. Specifically, the definition of *ReMembering* expands beyond memory to include the idea of becoming One or Whole again, threading the pieces of the Whole together. Awakening, too, is a form of ReMembering.

A glossary is included to help readers understand the definitions of some 'spiritual' terms used throughout this book. Most importantly, it gives the English definitions of many of the words used in the sacred Soul Language, Weeshah'aneylo.

It is also worth noting that all italicized quotes come from dimensions beyond our time and space. They are words spoken by those in the world of Shahalaku or by Spirit Guides from the Divine Realm.

This creative process of writing and receiving this story was intuitive and intentional. I called on Inner Knowing to guide these choices so that a transmission of Love from here and beyond may be felt and known at the deepest level.

I invite you to surrender to this journey and allow yourself to be transported out of this limited time-space dimension to feel the frequency from where these words originate. Receive the story from this timeless spaciousness, and you will experience the essence of its transmission entering your heart, transcending the critical mind.

May the following words ReMember us all.

Threading of the Soul

Aka Aka

Halanema Aku

Wee Shahala

Honi mali Kalima

Kaliwah Aku

The winds thread through the

dimensions that speak sacred tones

Breathing Oneness into the hearts of those lost

in the wild lands of forgetting

Telling the stories

that drench the heart

with soulful ReMemberings

I am never forgotten

I am free in Forever

I hold the fire

deep in my

Essence

and shine forth the Light

that threads the many

together

as One.

Introduction

Taka kakina wa'hah
Hōlimani wali'ha
Haka kakina ta ta ta taa

These words come from a space and place beyond time, beyond this dimension of deep density; from a world that knows no separation from others or Self. It holds the frequency of Wholeness and Creation, for it is unhindered by the fear-based energies that usurp our power, our trust in Self and Life Itself. This is the place from which I originate, a parallel world that I am ReMembering as I Awaken to a language that seems to be buried in my cells, my heart, and now emerges with a power and love that feels both foreign and familiar.

The energy of the voice that speaks in my native tongue transcends my current human inner chatter and my egoic thoughts and calls me to a spaciousness unhindered by the internal war, the tug and pull of contradictory polarities. From this spacious space, there is room to breathe, feel, and see something beyond. I can hear this voice emerging from the uncharted territory of my Soul. I sense guidance, a deep knowing, and a welling up of creative possibility. ~Beki

"Write a book, a fictional-true story, about the world that you inhabit in another time, space, and body. As you write, you will ReMember. It will carry the transmission of a world of Oneness lived in fullness. It will inject a frequency of this Wholeness into your time and space, Awakening those touched by this story to a Truth that lies in the Memory of their own Soul."

*"Do this, dear one, for **your** Awakening, for in Oneness, there is no other."*

"All are One
One is All
When I embrace
the heart of
the other
I am
whole."

~the voice from beyond the veil

PART ONE

THREADING OF THE SOUL

ONE

Land of Waterfalls

Hahti hahti halawa hahti
Hahti hahti pawcawa'ha

In a world of tomorrow, a long time ago, within the realm of the eternal now, there is a village nestled in the mountains, surrounded by waterfalls that bring abundance and beauty unparalleled to anything our remembered history has revealed. Each waterfall offers its unique qualities and gifts. Some pour forth a soft, warm flow of water that people in the village enjoy when they bathe their bare bodies in this rich and nourishing fluid. The water carries a scent of sweet exotic flowering plants that grow in the mountain's riverbeds. The souls of these plants merge with the beings they touch, and their magical aromas bring health and luminosity to their bodies. When the villagers emerge from these plant-infused waters, they glow from the inside out. It is a distinct and extraordinary gift.

Some waterfalls offer a powerful force that provides the energy needed to power the technologies that bring electrical frequencies into the villagers' dwellings. Of course, this electrical current is not to be compared to what we have become accustomed to in our time and space. The energy that comes from the waterfall carries the soul of this water and brings a harmonious pulsing frequency that activates the natural biorhythms within the sentient beings in the area. It bathes the energy fields of those engaging with the technologies it powers, providing an impulse of vitality and inspiration that, in turn, fuels innovation and creativity in the community.

Another one of the sacred waterfalls brings a cleansing and clearing quality to all living within the surrounding environment. Like a huge smudging instrument, the water and its movement can remove any disharmonious frequencies or elements, visible or invisible, from the environment. Its mist and energetic emanations powerfully create a clean and clear container for all those within its jurisdiction.

Each waterfall in the village is given a name. The inhabitants of this sacred land clearly understand that the water and its natural state of movement are not only sentient itself but are intimately attuned to the essence within each individual. They understand that these waterfalls are embodied Divine Beings, like themselves, and that, at the deepest level, they are a part of them. They innately know they are to the waterfall as the cells are to the water in their bodies. They understand that they are intrinsically and indistinguishably connected. They also know that all that is expressed in form in themselves and the world around them emerges from the Infinite, Eternal, formless One, and therefore, they are One with all and everything.

This idea of Oneness, a popular term in recent decades within spiritual circles of our time, is not a concept to the people of this time and space but a knowing, a given. It is a felt experience, simply and clearly understood — just as we know that fire is hot, or ice is cold. Here, in this world of waterfalls in a space beyond time a long time ago, *all* inhabitants, including the elementals, the mammals, and the space between, are of a consciousness that has not forgotten the Truth of Oneness. So much so that they can feel us now, here in our time and space, as an extension of their Being. They feel our despair as we flail amidst the consequences of forgetting this simple and undeniable Truth of Oneness.

Since we are One with them, and they have not forgotten, they reach out through dimensions to share with you the Memory. They whisper in the winds across time, of the eternal and timeless. They send the scent of sweet memories that open our hearts. They tickle the mind with ideas inspiring beauty expressed through the art of all forms. They blow out misty dew drops that we breathe in, moistening the erotic fire that makes us dance wildly to the sacred memory of fertility and passion. They sing sweet melodies into our dreams to Awaken us to our true nature of unparalleled beauty and intrinsic worth.

As we receive these invisible transmissions from the part of us that our minds have forgotten, we create masterpieces of this timeless knowing and surround ourselves with Beauty that penetrates the dense layers of pain and suffering that our forgetting has created.

It is time for us to bring our undivided focus to Beauty so that we can Awaken from this nightmare and return to the garden of waterfalls that seeks to cleanse our souls, sweeten the scent of our bodies, and nourish us with pulsations of vitality and inspiration. It is time to reclaim the Self and our Wholeness and choose what we *say* we desire. We have a choice. It is time to remember that!

TWO ⊙

Shahalaku Speaks

Awella'hah
Awella'ho
Shahalaku
Shahai'kiki

I am that I am
The Loving Self
Holder of Wisdom
Meeting the Truth

"I am known as Shahalaku, the Loving Self, and I live in the land of waterfalls.

"*Falling water brings life, movement, energy, and an abundance of gifts seen and unseen. I am a lover of the Self, the Divine Essence, who expresses through my being and lives in and animates all that is unfolding through form. I am a taste of your memory, lingering on your tongue, like a tingling sensation after consuming a perfectly spicy, hot pepper. I am the scent of the honeysuckle dancing with the hairs in your nostrils with a promise of sweetness beyond what is seen. I am the Self that lives with* nature: the beloved tall and majestic trees; the winding, wild vine draped with brightly colored blooms; the unassuming bud waiting to burst forth; the Earth-drenched roots ready to be consumed. I am the quiet, peaceful movement of big cats roaming the dense jungle. I am the flamboyant song of the cockatoo donning his crown of feathered glory. I am the Self fully expressed, fully known, undivided, and whole.

"In my world, we all live within this memory that you have forgotten. We have come through space and no-time to remind you of a Truth that will Awaken you to the Beauty that is You. We will tell the story of our world so you may feel the transmission of what is possible for you in the world of your time.

"Imagination is a function of creation. It is a quality within the mind that connects us to our Creator-Self. Imagination, which all beings possess when their souls first enter the physical body, is the quality of being that tethers us to our eternal and creative nature. It is the Divine Breath that breathes inspiration into our consciousness.

"Imagination is an abundant resource in our world of unparalleled Beauty and deeply tapped Wisdom. It is what allows us to effortlessly and joyously create the world we inhabit. We co-create this inner and outer world. Yet, this would assume that the 'other' is not a part of the I that is we. You see, in this land of Oneness, your breath is my breath. Your words are mine. Your wisdom lives in me. Your eyes see with my heart. My body speaks with your songs. We do not operate in a dimension of separation. Therefore, we must find a way to bridge our languages so that we may speak in a tongue you can perceive. But make no mistake, the utterances used to reach the human mind of your present time are only a translation of our language that has no words for 'you' or 'I.'

"We intend for the frequency of our native tongue to penetrate your language of 'other' so that we may infuse the Truth into that which we meet with Oneness. The voice of the one who narrates this story stands on the bridge between me, you, and we.

"Ahai kiki
Amundi'hah
Halawa hamini kiki
Wanima halawah'ha

Shall we begin…"

THREE

Imagination and Soul Memory

Hōkawa hakawa ha
Wah'halama nanya'ma ha

In the Land of Waterfalls, known as Hōlawai'kiki, which means *The Holy Waters to Which We Belong*, there lives a young woman of unique and alluring beauty. Her skin gleams like polished bronze. When the sun touches her face, it casts a radiant glow that bursts forth like starlight. She's tall and slender with a graceful, regal neck adorned with jewels of sparkly wonder. Her large, catlike eyes are yellow and green with dark indigo centers and curve around the side of her face dramatically. Her beautiful, golden-bronze, thick, soft locks cascade over her shoulders, brimming with an energy that contains magical properties of perception and wisdom.

Shahalaku is her name. She bears the mark of a Priestess: long, slender fingers embedded with the sacred, golden symbols of the healer's magic located in the place where others wear rings. She needs no rings, for she was born with these golden marks and knew her purpose before she could speak. Between each finger, a golden thread-like substance connects one digit to the next carrying a sacred frequency of energy that can be activated to initiate a healing ritual. It holds the ability to both receive and transmit

11

creating a current of energy for restoring balance and harmony in those she serves.

This organic technology, within these optic nerve-like threads, is more advanced than any technology created outside the physical body at any time or space. It is an expression of Oneness, unfragmented from its Source – a natural creation from this quality of Wholeness common to the land of Hōlawai'kiki. This particular expression is received by the souls who choose to be Hōwaka-heh/Priest/ess: those who gather the people in sacred ceremonies, offer healings and tend to people emerging from or returning to the *other place,* beyond the veil.

Imagination is a natural and sacred faculty of Creation, an intrinsic quality that all sentient beings of this land possess. However, some are particularly endowed with the art of imagination and express the wild and wondrous flavors of possibility in the sacred gatherings as a gift to stir the innate wisdom of imagination in others. Many of these beings are more recently incarnated yet old enough to have mastered the local dialect, Weeshah'aneylo. The young ones are more attuned to the untamed, spacious dimensions of the formless. One of the functions of these creative beings is to incite and inspire the community to continue to activate their faculty of imagination.

Another distinct quality of imagination is that it activates Soul Memory/ Wah'halama. The Soul, which presides beyond the consciousness of the incarnated self, holds the memories of all the multidimensional selves living in many different spaces, times, and bodies. Each being has a Soul that guides, directs, and contains the Whole Memory of all the expressions of Itself. This is the Self that is ReMembered and felt when allowing the imagination to reveal the Memory. Then, they would have access to all of the experiences and wisdom of all their selves, both embodied and formless.

The Soul (with an uppercase "S") is the OverSoul that sends forth, like offspring, extensions of Itself to be embodied in worlds of form so that It can experience Itself through the many diverse possibilities and realities available in the physical dimensions. The embodied soul (with a lowercase "s") is the unique expression born of the Essence of the Soul or OverSoul.

The soul receives impulses of guidance and awareness from its OverSoul to navigate the world of form that it inhabits. *Haa Whya Whoo* describes that which we have given many names: God, Source, Creator, Divine Love, Allah, Elohim, All That Is, Infinite One. Haa Whya Whoo gives birth to the many OverSouls and is, in a sense, the grandparent of the embodied soul. All of this is happening in no time, simultaneously, with the ability to be perceived sequentially. This construct allows for everything to slow down enough to enable the individual soul to savor the exquisite details of each experience within the Eternal Now.

Shahalaku loves to surround herself with the newcomers she helps usher in. She is continually inspired and renewed by their potent and visceral connection to the place beyond. She can feel the activation of her innate powers recharge when she touches the newborn with loving reverence and how they reawaken the memory of her own sacred origins. She especially loves to facilitate the ceremonies showcasing these wild ones who would describe colors, shapes, tastes, and textures that become fodder for the community to create new wonders to be experienced and explored.

The gatherings that the Hōwaka-heh preside over are varied. Some are filled with reverence and a depth of peace that bring the villagers into a state of intense communion with the formless dimension they call Ha'wahakakaya, most closely translated as a feeling of Pure Love within the Infinite Realm. The Creation Ceremony/Hōlimama-Fafui begins with emptying the mind of all that exists within form, creating a spaciousness to allow for the Ha'wahakakaya and its pure, raw energy of Love to penetrate the consciousness of the community. This activates the faculty of imagination, igniting a flame in the base of the skull.

This process allows access to both the individual OverSoul and the collective One Soul/Haa Whya Whoo, from which all Souls are birthed as distinct, unique expressions of the Infinite One. This Creation Ceremony/Hōlimama Fafui initiates a Collective Vision/Toka Maya to bring diverse qualities of individual creative expression into perfect harmony. Just as all the instruments played in an orchestra come together in a unified intention, bringing their unique sounds and vibrations to the

Whole, these ceremonies ignite a magnificent expression of Beauty for all to partake in.

It is only a matter of time before the manifestation of this Collective Vision finds its form in the physical world once activated from within this Infinite Field of imagination and creation. The idea of *believing in* or *trusting in* the fruition of this vision is foreign to those in this world. It is simply a knowing. The act of collective creation through sacred ceremony is so joyous and satisfying that the eventual outcome is not the focus. Creating is a communion between Pure Love Itself and the Eternal Soul. The pulsating force of unified creative frequencies, coursing through the minds and bodies of these beings, offers an ecstatic journey of untold proportions.

For Shahalaku, it is a profound honor to facilitate these ceremonies. She loves her post as Hōwaka-heh and seeks to cultivate and expand her craft daily with great love and enthusiasm. Another function she performs with her gift is to realign those who have wandered beyond their true nature into territories that take them out of balance with their Soul. This requires the skill of deep listening with both ears and hands. With intuitive attentiveness, she can pick up dissonant frequencies within the person that indicate a misalignment with their True Self. As she senses the subtle split of energy, she quickly initiates realignment with her electrically charged fingers.

Most cases require a simple entrainment with resonant frequencies for rebalancing. However, occasionally, a community member wanders into another dimension of time and space, introducing a frequency so foreign from their True Self that they would become cast under the spell of amnesia which is more common in the land of humans now. In these cases, she facilitates a cleansing ritual, clearing the attached energies that lower the natural buoyancy of knowing and memory.

Sometimes, she initiates a healing ritual within a magnetic chamber, charged with Earth crystals and star fragments, to restore balance and memory to the lost soul. In the center of this sacred space is a vessel filled with the water from the waterfall that clears imbalanced and dissonant frequencies from the land; this water is used to immerse the being. Using the beauty and power of her voice, Shahalaku sings ancient healing chants to remind them of their Wholeness. For the more stubborn cases of amnesia, Shahalaku works with the Council of Hōwaka-heh and sometimes calls on the community to surround the chamber and infuse the memory of Oneness into the afflicted.

Any illness that surfaces within this world is always a result of amnesia. It is rare for illness to take hold because the very nature of the beings of Hōlawai'kiki is to remember, to live in the memory of their connection to *All that Is* and to all Life that emerges from it. The very nature of their lives is a constant expression of this knowing.

Therefore, it is most common for her gifts to be utilized in ways that enhance the natural functions and expression of Oneness: for celebration rituals, sacred ceremonies, and tending to those birthing both in and out of the physical form. Shahalaku loves the expressions of her gifts and feels tremendous satisfaction for her Soul's decision to choose this vocation for her current embodiment.

FOUR

Transitions

Kini'hai kawahata
Hee tata mali mali'wah

Shahalaku is grateful for her life path as Hōwaka (short for Hōwaka-heh/Priest/ess) and loves to experience the energy and magic flowing through her for the benefit of all. She has but one sadness. She carries a hidden desire to bear children. While she loves being a facilitator of these sacred transitions, she also yearns to know the power and love that is unique to this experience. At the same time, she understands that this would not be in alignment with the gift she bears as Hōwaka. Her responsibility is to the Whole and to bring the individual into balance with the Infinite One. The energy required for her to tend to the entire community does not resonate with the gifts needed to be a wa'kamema/mother. Although the community as a whole is wa'keeda/parent to all children, the energy required to be the birthing parent both emotionally and physically would not allow for the fullness of her attention/toko-magua to her chosen vocation. This is a sacrifice she was willing to make, yet she did not expect this longing to persist.

Shahalaku pours herself into the joyful experience of creating a beautiful space for the kamema (short for mama) preparing for birth. It is one of her most beloved giftings, or hamanaku, which translates as "exchange of energy." She has an exquisite eye for beauty. The birthing chambers that she prepares in the homes of the kamema were always filled with color, teeming with blossoming plants and fragrant with healing aromas, creating the perfect gestation and birthing conditions for the unique needs and desires of both the mama and the soul about to emerge through her.

Shahalaku felt it was important to show the newly embodied soul the beauty of this land and to feel the activation of all its new senses as the baby entered. To know what the baby's soul desires, she and the pregnant woman go into the liminal field between worlds to connect with the consciousness of the unborn babe. This is how they receive specific guidance on how to prepare for the infant's arrival. This ceremony is profoundly moving and exciting to Shahalaku, for she is intimately attuned to the feeling of Oneness and can sense the Self in all beings, especially the new arrivals still tethered in fullness to their Higher Self, the True Essence of their being.

When a new one enters the community, there is a gathering of women who tend to the kamema and the child for many days after the birth. They are showered with gifts and love, stories of birthing and mothering, songs, and chants of celebration. Then, after the moon has completed an entire cycle, the villagers gather for a big feast to honor the new family member.

One of Shahalaku's most cherished songs for this celebration always brings her to tears: "*Hello friend, we have waited for you to return to us and bring back the wisdom of your voyage beyond our sight. We welcome you home, and we welcome the home that you have come from.*"

Tending to these life transitions gives her the fuel and energy to bring her full toko-magua/ focused attention to the ceremonial preparations for those on the path to reintegration with the Ha'wahakakaya/Infinite Realm of Pure Love. It required a very different he'kinika-hee/energy for her to tend to these beings. Unlike the world of humans of our time who often experience a painful sickness or a tragic accident as a way to make this transition, the people of Hōlawai'kiki consciously choose the time in which they will relinquish their body so that they can return to the Ha'wahakakaya. They feel the distinct calling of home from their Souls.

The ceremony for those departing their world begins with the leaders of the village gathering with the one who is making this transition asking, *"What do we have to know? What do you have to tell us?"*

Then, the children come and sing a chant, *"You will not be forgotten, neither your wisdom nor your courage. Your name will live forever amongst us."*

Then the men come and ask for a blessing, *"Please bless us, friend, before you must go, so that we can continue to grow and prosper in your absence."*

Finally, the women, those with magic in their hands, gather and begin to spread a cool cloth on that person, white for purity, and begin to scent the room with the minty, sweet aroma of hyssop blended with the piney, peppery scent of galangal. The women would sing songs of peace, songs of contentment, songs of unity, telling them: *"Do not fear; the walk is upon you. Begin this great exploration. There is so much to see and experience. We will miss you. We send each person's name with you so that you will remember them, and we shall keep your name in our hearts forever."*

The women would then offer up an anointing ceremony: *"We anoint the feet that will travel; we anoint the hands that will receive; we anoint the head that will know."* It is always a beautiful and moving celebration. Yet, there is still a deep mourning of not having this being within the physical world, especially for those closest in kin to the one making this transition. Therefore, Shahalaku and her fellow Hōwaka would tend to both the one going to the other place and those remaining. It is a very sacred role that Shahalaku artfully performs with great care and mastery.

The Hōwaka are given a great deal of respect and gracious appreciation by the community for their role in maintaining balance, harmony, and connection to the Loving Self and the Eternal One, which is central to the way of life in Hōlawai'kiki. So, while Shahalaku feels the yearning to be a wa'kamema at times, her life is primarily filled with her function as Hōwaka, which truly brings her great joy.

FIVE

Oneness and the One

Haa Whya Whoo
Haa Whya Whoo
Haa Whya Whoo

In the Land of Waterfalls, there is always an abundance of Beauty infused into the external world as well as the inner world of the inhabitants. It is teeming with life. Water is the greatest source of physical life. It is to the body what Love is to the Soul. It is what the body consists of and what sustains it. For the beings of Hōlawai'kiki, their relationship to the waterfalls is central to their way of life. It is clearly understood that they are so profoundly connected to the falling water that it is no less a part of them than their limbs or their organs.

This understanding is pervasive in their experience of life as intrinsically connected and essentially one with the Infinite One. Therefore, everything is part of the Whole, seen and unseen. The scent of the flower is a part of the flower. It is a characteristic of its nature, just as all beings expressed in physical form are a particular characteristic or quality of the Infinite One/Haa Whya Whoo. The taste of the fruit is a delicious expression of the essence of this specific fruit. All is a distinct expression of Haa Whya Whoo. Each time one speaks this word, it transmits the Eternal, Divine Love of the One Source into the person speaking it and hearing it, and it feels sublime.

The sound of "haaaa," if extended with a soft out-breath, is the frequency of Love embodied. This sound is infused into their language. It means *"Sacred Breath"* and is the closest term for what we call Love. It is a recognition that the Love of the One is being received when inhaling the Sacred Breath, also known as Ha'mana, and sent back out with each exhale. This simple, innate function of life, the breath, is a demonstration of Oneness, with each breath becoming a part of all Life as it circulates through the Whole. Haa Whya Whoo also can mean "Home of the Sacred Breath/the Sacred Breath is Home." With almost all the words ending in an out-breath, the language also functions to activate the Ha'mana/Sacred Breath, supporting the natural balance and Wholeness within the physical body and soul. For the breath is the Holy One becoming form. It is the fuel for creation.

Weeshah'aneylo, the language of the Sacred Breath, is also known as the language of Wholeness and Creation. The very frequency of the words themselves holds the essence of these qualities, just as the essence of a jasmine flower carries a distinct aroma, shape, and color. Each being and all life-forms have their unique essence that ultimately is an extension of the Higher Self and the Infinite One. The expression becomes more and more refined and distinct as it is developed at an individual level, offering their unique gifts. Each individual's physicalized expression contains particular desires that offer an even more unique flavor to be shared and experienced by the Self and the Whole.

There is immense value in both the experience of the Infinite One and that of the many layers of individuation. While the One is the Source of all the expressions, Its boundless parts extend forth, each engaging in their own manner of expression. This forms a magnificent web of the Divine Essence becoming more: evolving, creating, expressing, expanding, and ultimately returning to the One. This is the power and beauty of Being, giving birth to the endless desire for expansion and evolution. Each soul, and the life-forms they embody, enhance and augment the Source of All that Is.

Because this is deeply known by the beings of Hōlawai-kiki, they understand the sacred and precious nature of their existence, so their value is never in question. It's simply understood that their presence, life force, and the gifts they offer, that are unique to them, are an essential part of the Whole. They also feel this way about all other life-forms within creation. Because of this basic understanding, they have no need to be like anyone else to feel they belong. This concept would not even enter their minds.

SIX

The Body

Wehee tanyata ah'who ah Hōlawai

The body of the Hōlawai, as they referred to themselves, is as much a creative expression of their Soul Essence as it is an organic, physical expression of the Collective Vision/Toka Maya. Because of their undivided relationship to their True Self, they do not identify with the form they animate *as* the Self. They consider it an expression of their creation. They hold it with sacred reverence and enthusiastic appreciation. They love their bodies.

Hence, a great variety of physical qualities are expressed, and not one person fully resembles another unless this is the intention. They possess the essential human physical attributes, as we do. Yet, they all operate at a super-human level since they are not poisoned by environmental or mental toxins. Moreover, they do not possess the same limitations, mentally or physically, that we do. They don heads of hair with all textures, colors, and styles. Like humans of our time, hair is a greatly prized attribute of the body and is used for extraordinarily creative self-expression. The shades and textures of their skin also vary. Their bodies are as diverse as our flowering plants' vast and unique presentations.

Since they are incredibly talented at accessing the faculties of imagination, which include Soul Memory/ Wah'halama and creativity, along with knowing their connection to the Infinite Source of Creation, they are not limited in any way in molding a body of their choosing. In Hōlawai-kiki, there is such diversity that not one body is the same, making it externally and intrinsically evident that they each bring their unique gift to the Whole. They do not make comparisons with each other in ways that may cause a sense of jealousy because they have not forgotten that they have *chosen* the form they animate. However, they may be inspired by the attributes of another to use as ideas for self-expression to enhance their own form. This is considered a sign of great respect and appreciation. Also, they do not mistake their form as their identity. That would be like identifying with the painting or meal that you created as *who* you are. The body is a work of art you create from your Soul Essence. It is considered an expression of love, creation, and wholeness.

Hence, each being loves what they have created as their body. Everyone considers themselves beautiful at the very core. Yet, each individual holds a different idea of what beauty is. For instance, one may consider soft, small facial features alluring, and another may appreciate a bolder, more dramatic, angular facial structure. Another may value the quality of strength and large muscles, while another would prefer to be petite with an agile frame. No one is limited by their genes. because some of the basic characteristics passed through bloodlines are a part of how the Soul would consider which bodies would offer the appropriate seeds for inception. The qualities of the Soul Essence and how their parents provide their gifts to the community would also determine the prebirth choice of each soul.

It must be understood that the children, once born, become a part of the whole community and are cared for by the collective in various ways. Also, their creativity is supported by the body they are born into. They quickly realize they can transform it in ways we have not dreamed of if they feel it needs to be altered to serve a particular desire. Because of their uncorrupted relationship to the soul-self, OverSoul, and the Infinite One, their abilities are only limited by their imagination. For this reason, they are immediately encouraged to use the sacred faculty of imagination for shifting and molding the desired form.

A soul rarely chooses a form of limitation within the body. However, when this does happen, it is always understood that it is for the purpose of creation and experience on both the individual and collective levels. The Hōlawai consider these souls a unique gift to the community, as they understand the courage and creativity it takes to consciously choose limitations. They offer extra care to support the new child in attuning to the body and help them stay aware of why they have chosen this physical expression. Therefore, no one ever feels like a victim of the form they embody.

SEVEN

The Young

Dyastina kanyatta hah'ku oh Hōlawai
He'nyanama hokawah'hani
Hah'tinawah hakawha hai

Shahalaku and her fellow Hōwaka are guides to those in charge of reminding the young of what they already know. This is the closest thing they have to what we call teachers. Their primary function is not so much to teach, but rather to remind. These beings choose to use their gifts to guide the children to stay awake to their innate knowing as they attune their consciousness to the physical mind and body, which can be so deliciously distracting – just as it is for us in our dimension.

Some specific vital questions and rituals reactivate their memory and ability to tap into their Soul's knowing. Questions such as: Who are you? Who do you choose to be? What quality of experience do you choose to have? Why have you chosen this form/ this time/ this space to be embodied? They discuss with them the different qualities of Being such as loving, helpful, kind, strong, resilient, intelligent, thoughtful, philosophical, ambitious, inventive, creative, flexible, adaptable, inquisitive, adventurous, etc. They may prompt them with questions such as: What part of the Whole would you like to be expressed through you, and how does it reflect your distinct essence? How can you bring this unique flavor, scent, and frequency of yourself to these attributes you choose to experience?

The questions offer an opportunity to contemplate what the being came to experience in this unique time and space. Once the memory is activated and understood at a mental level in the person, they can easily access all information needed to mold their self-expression.

The concept of education as we know it would be absurd to them. They are not meant to simply receive the information already known by those sharing it, whether inscribed in books or shared through stories. They are inspired to create a *new* expression of Life through them. Therefore, the information could be more of a distraction than support until they have fully formed that which they choose to be, experience, and create. After they have done so, information, stories, and support from the experiences of others can be of great value to help the being develop and create that which they are choosing.

So, at a very young age, children are encouraged to become aware of their unique essence and explore how they may choose to express themselves. For the Hōlawai, it would be unthinkable to suppress their self-expression. Self-expression is a way in which they offer their gifts to the Whole. It is how they are able to experience the exchange of energy that is essential and natural to the continuation of Life. Spending most of their time ingesting information/knowledge from the known dimension would hinder the individual's development in accessing the knowing of their Soul. The resource of Knowing, at this level, is profoundly superior to any information offered through the collective mind embodied at any given time period. For the Soul contains memory and wisdom that spans all time and space of the multidimensional self.

Each embodied soul carries unique wisdom born of experiences that only it would know and be able to transmit to the collective. So, "education" would emphasize supporting the new ones in reconnecting to their infinite wisdom and inner knowing and finding creative ways to bring it forth into their chosen experiences in their current existence. As such, the activation of their Soul's purpose, which they came to offer as their gift, would be very quickly activated and expressed.

Therefore, institutions of learning are simply not required. Once the person reconnects their awareness to the True Source of wisdom and knowing, the need for the cumbersome and time-consuming drills for learning, memorization, and regurgitation of information is unnecessary.

They can access unlimited knowledge when tuned in and aligned with their Soul's wisdom. Not only can they retrieve deep understanding and wisdom due to their own multidimensional experiences in all time and space, but they can also access the collective knowing ensouled by the Infinite One. While one being would not access *all* information at once, they could retrieve what was needed when desired. Therefore, memorization, as we know it, is entirely unnecessary.

You can see that the need for an artificial intelligence (AI) system to house all the information at the level of form is unnecessary, as such a system could never be as unlimited as the Infinite Source of All. This infinite database, which we call the Akashic Records (AR), is available to all. The Hōlawai have always retained the inner technology that gives them access to this Source.

In our world of today, there is an epidemic of memory loss. Diseases that rob the memory are reflections of a more profound loss of the memory of our True Self that is Infinite, Pure, Divine Love incarnate. After eons of this sustained collective amnesia, it is no wonder that we would suffer from the loss of memory with diseases such as dementia and Alzheimer's. It is time to Awaken to the profound power that resides within.

This is the purpose of this transmission: to remind us of a deeper Truth that many of us are sensing stirring within us, tickling us, to Awaken.

EIGHT

Truth

Mai haya'nata
Ki maya'hata
Ki'waha iōway nani mali'wah

The philosophy, understanding, or knowing of the Hōlawai is innately understood and does not require teaching. It arises from an inner space of a felt knowing of the Soul's Truth rather than from *believing* a particular thing. They rarely use the word "knowledge," which we refer to as information. Instead, they express a knowing that comes from a deep, intuitive place of understanding. This knowing does not require consensus because it is understood that each being has their own authority from which they receive this knowing. It is not only expected but celebrated that the relative truths, born of deep knowing, are varied and diverse. These personal truths serve as a compass to direct each being through physical life in a way that aligns with their Soul Blueprint, which outlines the themes and intentions mapped out prior to birth. The closest concept to a consensus agreement on a truth being true would be the idea of *resonance*. Groups of individuals gravitate toward each other to congregate in communion based on this felt sense of resonance. Sometimes, these groups may even choose to live in the same dwelling.

This means that the birth family may or may not be the family of resonance where one would choose to live. Yet, the love for all community members is felt and honored even if one does not resonate with the particular truth of another. Love and resonance are not necessarily synonymous. Since the diversity of self-expression in all ways is encouraged and celebrated, to expect or even desire that everyone believes or knows the same thing as true would be a contradiction. It is understood that individual truths are an extension of Divine Creation, as well as a ReMembering of one's Soul Knowing.

In other words, they know that they are both individually and collectively creating truth as a way to experience a particular reality in form. This created truth is inspired by the Divine Truth and serves Creation, but once it is interpreted at the level of form, it is relative truth. Therefore, they are not bound to these truths, for they are mutable and moldable. When they no longer serve the individual or the community, they simply choose to create, through their unlimited imagination, a truth that would be more efficient at producing the experience they then desire.

For instance, they would never choose to create a truth that offers an experience of their food as toxic to their bodies. Likewise, they could not conceive of creating a reality in which their environment or other beings would be dangerous to their well-being (i.e., pollutants, chemicals, viral or bacterial pathogens, etc.). Certainly, they would not dream of using the sacred faculty of imagination to create a reality in which the touch or breath of one person could be a cause of harm to another. For in their world, water and breath are the essence of the body and soul. Water is the main composition of the body. Breath is the life force and energy of the OverSoul that sustains the embodied soul and enlivens the physical body. The intermingling of the body and breath with another is the sacred acknowledgment of the immutable Divine Truth: *All are One, One is All. When we embrace the heart, breath, and water of another, we are made Whole.*

To forget this intrinsic and Ultimate Truth is to sink into the illusion common in the dimensions in which amnesia has taken hold of minds that no longer know they are the creators of their lives.

NINE

The Infinite One,
OverSoul, Soul, and soul

Wah'halama wa'ki takunama ha
Ha'mana iōwayah'ho
Haa Whya Whoo

It is understood by the Hōlawai that the Sacred Breath of the Soul is the source of their creative energy and life force. As previously shared, the individual soul is an expression and extension of the Higher Self, the Soul or the OverSoul. The OverSoul is the unique expression and extension of the Infinite One or All that Is. This is what they collectively have agreed upon as true. It is a construct born of a deeper knowing and Soul Memory/ Wah'halama. Yet, all constructs are created to offer an opportunity for particular experiences. It is an enduring construct that has served the desires of the collective, and therefore, it has become a pillar of truth or understanding within their community. While it may be considered a belief from the current human perspective, it is regarded as a *truth* because it was created through collective imagination derived from the Collective Wah'halama. All agree it is true because the collective created this truth in harmony with the Whole. They recognize that they are a part of this consciousness of knowing.

Since the Hōlawai are so attuned to their source of wisdom, the truths that emerge from collective imagination are profoundly felt and known in a very direct way. It is as tangible to them as holding an apple. They are given guidance to attune to the energy of the physical world but never forget the quality and nature of the non-physical signature of their own distinct vibration.

They never experience amnesia within the dimension of reality they inhabit However, they understand that if, at some point, they *choose* amnesia, another aspect of their Higher Self could project an extension of Self, as another soul, (an aspect of the multidimensional Self) into another time/space and body to have that experience. The possibilities for Life experiencing Itself are unlimited.

It is deeply understood and honored that this world of Hōlawai'kiki will continue to hold a frequency of ReMembered Oneness and will be a beacon of Light for those who may choose to venture beyond this Land of Wholeness and Creation into more dense dimensions of reality. For an embodied soul, it can be a place of restoration and joyous creativity.

Shahalaku loves to share stories and facilitate rituals in community gatherings. They offer rich fodder to colorfully and creatively activate the innate memory that originates from their OverSoul connecting them to their multidimensional selves who are living lives within different dimensions of time and space. It is a co-creation with all beings present, each sharing their way of ReMembering with the Whole. It is individual memories that make up the Whole and the communion with the One that activates these memories. These gatherings offer an opportunity to enjoy the beautiful and diverse ways in which the One expresses in form and consciousness. It is a grand celebration that honors the All and everyone present.

TEN

Multidimensional Self

Maya'halawa hah'taa
Wah'halama iōwayah'ho-kiki

While Shahalaku adores her life in this beautiful, harmonious Land of Waterfalls she can also feel a longing for another experience calling her. So, one day, as she communed with her Higher Self, she engaged her imagination specifically to explore the possibilities for her to experience another incarnation within her multidimensional Self.

She understood what all those in her land knew: that time is an illusion and that all possibilities and incarnations are happening in Hah'laqua/the Eternal Moment of Now. Therefore, the world of Shahalaku is unfolding simultaneously and concurrently with ours. Considering this, we could as easily be speaking in the present moment as in the past when describing the life and world she inhabits. It is a natural and organic dance within sharing this ReMembering because, in truth, there is only NOW.

Shahalaku enjoyed the adventure of exploring the lifetimes of her parallel selves or soul-kin/iōwayah'ho-kiki. In one life, she was a Portuguese Priest living in Japan in the 1400s, who made the study of language a method of connection. He was fluent in 16 languages and had great agility with another seven. His skills allowed him to be an excellent counselor with people of different ethnicities and cultures. He had formed such strong alliances that he became a diplomat in Japan. As a result, he developed a special relationship with the Emperor's son and taught him Portuguese. This young man believed he was a soldier and pursued this life with great determination, but it did not fit him. He was chasing the dreams of others and could not understand why he did not progress as his peers did. It was not until he met the Priest and embarked on the spiritual path, that was first fomented by a love of language, that he began to see another life for himself.

As Shahalaku pondered her life as the Portuguese Priest and his special bond with this young man, another intriguing lifetime was revealed. She recognized herself as a beautiful, dark-haired woman who was considered a witch. Because her powers frightened the people in her world, she had learned to live as discreetly as possible. As a young woman, she was abducted by a trained soldier. He was a vassal of a nobleman who had tasked him to find the heir of the holder to the title of the Forbidden Lands. The nobleman wanted the land for himself and would do anything to ensure no one would dispute his claim. The genuine claimant of the land was known to have a distinct mark on his back. The soldier had heard of the witch's powers and forced her to help him. They traveled for nine months, during which time they became close and fell in love. When they consummated their love, he discovered the mark on her back and realized that she was the true claimant of this land. He then switched his allegiance to the witch and helped her restore her claim to the land.

Shahalaku was fascinated by this relationship and felt a flutter in her heart as she viscerally witnessed their love for each other. She marveled at how their unlikely union transformed the shortsightedness of the soldier who assumed the claimant was a man or perhaps a baby. A person bonded to the Earth can only see what is. His original thoughts were that witches were evil, but then he fell in love and married her. Although his vision was initially small, his partnership with this woman, guided by an alternative way, allowed him to reach his true purpose.

This exploration of the lives of her soul-kin, another part of her own Soul, expanded her consciousness and filled her heart with awe. Yet, it was not until her awareness landed in a space and time within our Earthly now that she was certain she had found the experience she yearned for. She felt a pull towards a woman known as *Beki*, who possessed certain qualities that particularly resonated with her. She observed that this being was a creative thinker and uninterested in fitting into the constructs of reality common for her time and place on Earth. She questioned the knowledge fed to her by society and sought a more profound knowing that came from within. She loved to create art that arose from her Soul, whether with words or paint. From the broader perspective of her OverSoul, Shahalaku could see how Beki's life was filled with love and beauty and that she had chosen to experience the challenges and richness of motherhood as a powerful way to expand and evolve. Like Shahalaku, she was a lover of the Divine and yearned to commune with her True Self.

Shahalaku especially appreciated how Beki was able to experience both mothering and the expression of her unique, creative, divine nature through her work as an artist and energy healer. She recognized the soldier's soul, in her life as a witch, embodied again with Beki as her beloved, her husband, and the father of their three sons. Sensing this enduring union throughout lifetimes sent sweet, sensual ripples of energy through Shahalaku's body.

At that moment beyond time, with great excitement, Shahalaku decided to infuse her presence and distinct essence into this alternate reality in a way that would enhance both beings who were expressions of their shared OverSoul. Simultaneously, she released all expectations of how this meeting of souls would unfold, for she knew that this would hinder the flow of the broader perspective of the Higher Self to bring forth the perfect scenario and conditions to allow this meeting to occur in a way that would benefit All. Her excitement and eager anticipation overflowed with joy.

She had complete faith that the magic had begun.

ELEVEN

Namundhi

Xanlahmundhi pah'kuwha
Su'halamista
Ku'awa Haa

One day, as Shahalaku was deeply absorbed in her meditation, communing with her Higher Self, she felt the quiet, wise presence of her mentor and fellow Priestess, Namundhi, standing at the threshold of her sacred dwelling. She patiently waited as Shahalaku completed her ritual and then came in and sat across from her on the velvety red cushion ornately embroidered with turquoise and fuchsia yarn.

Shahalaku bowed with reverence and affection. *"Welcome, teacher; what brings you to my abode?"* she asked, as Namundhi settled into the cushion. She was pleasantly surprised by her presence and knew to expect a delicious exchange and opportunity for growth.

Namundhi's face shone with the deep red-bronze tones that reflected Shahalaku's skin. It was Namundhi who had inspired her to adopt this distinct texture and tone for her own skin. It was regal and inviting all at once. The reflective quality of her skin had a magical way of mirroring the essence of another allowing them to see their beauty more clearly.

Namundhi also had wooly locks that fell over her shoulders and bore the traditional golden mark of the Priestess embedded on her long, slim fingers. Her warm eyes matched the bronze tones in her hair. Her nose was broad, and her lips were full, with her two front teeth prominently displayed when she smiled, which was most of the time. This was an endearing quality and considered a sign of beauty in Hōlawai'kiki. She wore an oversized green gemstone on one ear. Although her mentor had lived much longer than herself, she was stunning. Deterioration of the physical body is not a part of aging in Hōlawai'kiki. Namundhi's appearance had been a significant source of inspiration for Shahalaku in the creative expression of her own physical body.

Namundhi leaned forward and kissed Shahalaku on her forehead with motherly love, and with excitement, she began to share. Her words danced from her lips with a lilting, poetic rhythm that mesmerized Shahalaku, requiring her to fully engage her toko-magua/focused attention to concentrate on what she was saying.

Namundhi had just come from a ritual fasting and ceremonial communion with her OverSoul, in which she had become attuned to a Soul Memory of an exchange that her soul was having with a woman from another time and space where there was great turmoil and transformation. This person turned out to be another incarnation of Shahalaku who was seeking guidance from a psychic medium on how she could best be of service at that time.

Shahalaku's iōwayah'ho-kiki/soul-kin was an artist and energy healer assisting her clients in remembering their Infinite Divine Selves. She was sitting in a small, cozy room filled with colorful paintings that she had created. They vibrated with an energy and luminosity reminiscent of Shahalaku herself. This is how Namundhi knew who she was for sure.

Namundhi began to describe this woman, who called herself Beki. *"She has reddish-brown skin warmed by the sun's rays and her soft brown curls, with wisps of white around her hairline, come to her shoulders. Her body is much smaller than the average woman here, and her facial features are more subtle and refined than yours. While her self-expression is much less dramatic than most of us, she possesses her own unique beauty and flair that reflects the essence of your shared Soul. She was wearing turquoise on her ears and fingers with a simple, clear quartz crystal on a silver chain draped around her neck that you would have loved. She bears a beauty-mark above her lip that mirrors the one you yourself have in the very same place!"* Namundhi reached to touch Shahalaku's face pointing to her beloved mark.

Namundhi had felt that this was a wonderful opportunity for her to interject her presence and wisdom to offer Beki support. She continued to describe how she witnessed Beki speaking with Myrna, the medium, who had the gift of receiving and translating the presence and messages of non-physical entities. Through a small screen, Beki was sharing with Myrna how before getting on the call she had been contemplating who she may want to connect with, from the other side, when she sensed pressure around her throat and heard her inner voice say, *"You will meet someone new today."* Beki wondered who this might be. This was when Myrna became aware of Namundhi, who had been energetically brushing her fingers across Beki's throat to get her attention. Once her presence was acknowledged, Namundhi was able to have a conversation with Beki through the medium which felt like a very long time, although in linear time was only one hour.

Shahalaku listened intently, with recognition and awe, not wanting to interrupt Namunhi's recount of her exchange with the very being that she herself had already become aware of just days before.

"I decided I would help her remember our language of Wholeness and Creation. It can be of great benefit for us to infuse the frequency of Weeshah'aneylo (their language) into her time when most beings are held captive by a very stifling frequency of separation consciousness, caused by amnesia.

"Remember the ones who have traveled to these denser dimensions of forgetfulness? It takes great effort for us to restore their memory of Wholeness. Sometimes, they even carry back painful and often debilitating conditions in their bodies that are called 'diseases' in this land that Beki inhabits. She is following the inner guidance that has called her to help others remember so they can heal. She seems sincere in her desire to grow

her abilities to truly serve her people's Awakening. She is very much a part of you, Shahala, and she is willing to receive our language to ReMember. I told her I would walk part of the way with her to help her reclaim her native tongue. Can you sense her? Can you feel yourself in this world of chaos? How can we bring what we know to this intense time for humanity? I am not embodied in this time and space, but your iōwayah'ho-kiki is. How brave for this part of you to choose such a time to incarnate. I am told that many souls are choosing embodiments within this dimension and time on Earth to raise consciousness enough to abate a great planetary catastrophe. This is a significant yet exciting challenge.

"It is known that the possibility of an extinction of most mammalian life on Earth could occur within just decades from the time she/you inhabit. Most of the bodies of humans have been impacted by toxins that, for some, are causing horrific pain and suffering. Since they have forgotten that they are one with the Source of all life they do not feel they have a choice on what the experience to a great degree. There are endless wars between nations that pale in comparison to the inner wars that these humans wage within their own minds. They are not only divided between each other but within their very being.

*"They rarely **choose** to go to the other side because they are terrified and believe that they will die. So, they unconsciously create opportunities to leave the body, which, of course, is necessary for their evolution. Yet it then makes them feel as though they are victims of life. They do not understand that they create their life experiences and that this is a gift. This world would be unfathomable to those in Hōlawai'kiki. However, a great and quiet revolution of Awakening is underway. It is a very exciting and tense time. I feel that we can help!"*

Namundhi's enthusiasm was contagious. She was passionate about the Awakening of humanity and knew that the frequencies within their sacred language would be a potent elixir for initiating this Awakening. As she spoke, Shahalaku could feel the stirring of this part of her Soul, the human–soul who was embodied in this strange world of separation and polarity — a world of beings who were deeply asleep, in a state of amnesia. She could sense Beki's fatigue and feelings of isolation. She could feel the pangs of her worry. These emotional sensations were foreign to Shahalaku, yet a ReMembering connected her to her other selves, living lives that were less harmonious and attuned to Oneness than her own life. At the same time, Shahala could also feel Beki's strength, creativity, and passion for life, which reminded her of herself. It was a curious sensation – these polarized frequencies within one being. She also could feel Beki's devotion to the Divine with a deep desire to help others who were suffering from their own state of forgetfulness. While she tuned into the blossoming journey of Beki's Awakening, she could also feel her clinging to the conditioned mind that suppressed her full ReMembering.

Shahalaku felt this invitation from both the part of herself dwelling in this world of separation and the mentor she so admired. Namundhi eagerly shared possible ways that they could engage with Beki to assist in her desire to serve the Awakening to Divine Love and Oneness in herself and the world she inhabited. Of course, she knew that this meeting was an orchestration of her Higher Self, creating the opportunity and path for communion with Beki, whom she had already chosen to experience for her own evolution. The initiation of this desire and intention had occurred simultaneously just as Namundhi was co-creating from her own shared desire to be a source of Awakening. After all, her personal number was nine, known as Doosh'dahah Aho, which translates as *Awaken Now*.

With great enthusiasm, Shahalaku shared with Namundhi how she had explored the unique lives of several of her soul-kin living in other dimensions. She described her reasons for choosing Beki with whom to deepen her connection. She was delighted by the way her Higher Self facilitated the initiation of this reunion with her iōwayah'ho-kiki by incorporating her beloved mentor to be a part of this journey. She was over the moon with gratitude, for she could not have imagined a better approach to entering the domain of density and separation in a way that she would feel so supported than to be accompanied by Namundhi. Together, they marveled with joy and awe at the creativity of the Infinite!

TWELVE

Creation Ceremony and Soul–Kin

Hōlimama Fafui
Hee nani maliwah
Iōwayah'ho-kiki
Wanahaa hee toko-magua Hah'laqua

The technology of the Hōlawai is an exquisite blend of elegant simplicity with highly advanced capabilities that perform in service of their extraordinary ideas for creative manifestations. While function is essential to its purpose, attention to aesthetic details is essential for the expression and experience of Beauty, which is central to all that they create. They understand the importance of the vibrational frequencies that Beauty expresses in creation and what it offers to the beings and the land they belong to. It is akin to the merging of lovers in the sacred act of sexual union/hōlamakini. When the feminine Love of Beauty/Wanahaa meets the masculine energy of focused attention/toko-magua in a passionate embrace, creation is imminent.

This balance between the masculine and feminine energies is an essential aspect of the ceremony that the Hōwaka-heh/Priest/esses facilitate for collective creation. As the community enters the Ha'wahakakaya (the

Infinite Realm), it is like going into the dark womb, empty and full of possibility, holding the profoundly sacred frequency of creation. This is the feminine quality of Wanahaa infused with the beauty of the life force, the breath of life. Once they all reach a state of empty mind held within the spaciousness of Infinite Possibility Possibility, the Hōwaka-heh guide them to activate their collective imagination with toko-magua/focused attention — the masculine quality, the breath of creation and manifestation. This union of energies initiates an opening of collective and individual Soul Memory / Wah'halama that reaches beyond the embodied soul to the Higher Self. Finally, this activation allows access to the Infinite One, the Creator of All.

In a sense, these ceremonies are like the whole community making Love for the Collective Creations. This is how all the wisdom and information for their technologies were received and then created. It is a profoundly exciting process. The passion and ecstasy of this union with the Divine levels of consciousness within themselves, each other, and the Infinite is indescribable.

The sacred act of sexual union/hōlamakini, experienced with a couple in the creative act of Love, Beauty, and Creation, is a microcosm of this more communal act which brings its own unique experiences of sensual and physical ecstasy. For the Hōlawai, every act is full of the frequency of Love. Love is the highest expression of the self which aligns one to the Soul. Because Wholeness and Creation are so intrinsic to the Hōlawai, they would only consider doing something with the infusion of Love, which is the essence of the creation process. They understand its power and how it assures the balance, harmony, and beauty of all that they create.

Not long after their meeting, Shahalaku and Namundhi decided to initiate a Creation Ceremony/Hōlimama Fafui with just the two of them to activate their faculty of imagination to align with the Wah'halama/Soul Memory. This would enable them to become more receptive to insights on how best to offer their love and support to Shahala's soul-kin/iōwayah'ho-kiki embodied as Beki in this alternate reality. As they emerged from the ceremony, they discussed what they had each received and excitedly designed a plan of action.

They decided that Namundhi would communicate directly with Beki through Myrna, the Mystic Medium, who had translated her words faithfully on their first meeting. It was imperative that Beki prompt these meetings and allow the messages to come to her of her own Free Will/Aweesha. Otherwise, she could not fully and accurately receive the transmission of the frequency from the Hōlawai language, Weeshah'aneylo. Once the language Awakens in her, with her distinct energetic permission, and the inner activation of this memory, Beki would be able to perceive the messages directly from Shahalaku. For, in essence, the two are one. Beki has a strong resonance with the understanding of Oneness, and throughout her lifetime, she has been drawn to the spiritual teachings that embody the wisdom of this Truth. If Beki is receptive, there will be an open window for her to accept this hamanaku/exchange between beings (a.k.a. vocation/career/dharma/purpose), allowing her to embody the distinct frequency of Weeshah'aneylo so she can transmit their gifts into her time.

"Imagine, Shahala, what we can accomplish using what we know and so effortlessly embody in our world and then transmit this energy to your iōwayah'ho-kiki in this other reality!" Namundhi exclaimed.

Shahalaku was reeling with ideas and mesmerized by the powerful and graceful energy of her friend and fellow Hōwaka-heh, who had mentored her and initiated her into developing her gift of hamanaku since she was a child. Now that Namundhi had accepted the call to be her Life Path Guide in another time and space, Shahala felt the fullness of her mentor's Love and commitment to herself as Shahala *and* Beki as well as to the Awakening of All in all time and space. She was overcome with gratitude and tenderness for this great and generous Soul that Namundhi embodied. She also felt the Oneness within this entire creative allowing. The union of aspects of the Whole intermingling Its consciousness in this extraordinary exploration of creative, sacred service felt utterly exhilarating. This was the ecstasy of merging the Wanahaa and toko-magua (Love of Beauty and Focused Attention). It was sublime. It is what she loves so much about being Hōlawai within this time and space.

As she contemplated her appreciation for the way of the world she inhabited, she felt a growing sense of compassion and Love for the part of her Soul that inhabited the dimension wrought with strife and separation. The inspiration to bring her unique Love and wisdom to this time caused her heart to well up with excitement at the possibilities. This would be a wonderful exploration of how Love can be felt and expressed beyond dimensions.

She felt her whole being and body tingle with anticipation of making contact with this aspect of her Beloved Self.

THIRTEEN

Awakening Beki

Doosh'dahah Aho palku palku palku
Hah'laqua makinwa'ha

In contemplating how and when Shahalaku would make contact with Beki, there was much to be considered. First and foremost, it was critical to offer only a frequency that could be felt and sustained by the human soul, Beki. If it was too much too soon, it could have a detrimental impact on her physical and mental bodies. Since the Hōlawai live in a world where "time" as we know it does not exist, they could use this to their advantage. The Hōlawai know, experientially, the organic technologies based on the emerging understanding of Quantum Physics in our time. Using this information, Namundhi and Shahalaku prepared a sequence of impulses to occur within Beki's lifetime that would gradually Awaken her memory of Divine Truth. This would offer a gentle infusion of the frequencies of Oneness from the soul-self embodied as Shahalaku into the body and mind of the soul-self embodied as Beki.

In Quantum reality, it is understood that everything is happening in the Eternal Moment of Now/ Hah'laqua. Past, present, and future are constructs for linear, sequential "time" to be experienced. However, in truth, time is a measurement used to describe the movement from one *now* to another *now*, both of which are already in existence — just as the world of form exists simultaneously with the formless dimension. It does not simply emerge when you enter the new realm of reality. It is present now, and when you become aware of it, it emerges as *your* experience of reality. You realize — with *real eyes* — what is already there. It is a matter of shifting frequencies to be able to actually perceive this alternate reality so that you can *experience* it. When a child is born into form, entering from the formless, she is simply revealed to the dimension of reality that was previously invisible to her. Yet the reality already existed within the Infinite Realm of possibility. This is the case for all perceivable realities. This is a function of consciousness: to perceive and experience infinite expressions of reality, one at a time.

This is why the Hōlawai do not consider an alternate embodiment of their Soul as a past or future lifetime. This term is relative to the perception of linear time experienced by humans on Earth Beki's time. While the Hōlawai are highly evolved beings within the Earth plane, they do not inhabit the same frequency as humans living in the time of separation consciousness. Therefore, their existence would not be easily perceivable to humans in this dimension. Those on Earth "today" who speak of a "New Earth," a more Utopian world, are actually sensing a reality that is already now. But, since it is vibrating at a frequency so different from the Earth and consciousness they know, they can only perceive it based on their particular level of sentience: the degree to which the individual or collective is aligned to the frequency of their OverSoul.

The Hōlawai are highly attuned to this Soul frequency, not just at the individual Soul/OverSoul level but also at the level of the Infinite One. These frequencies of consciousness contain an exquisite quality of knowing and creative potential. Thus, they are not restricted by the limitations of humans who are hindered by this inner and outer division from the self and All that Is. This separation consciousness has precipitated a tendency to identify themselves as the matter they embody rather than the Soul Essence that utilizes the potent gift of Divine Energy to activate and direct matter.

Very few humans have been able to communicate with the world of the Hōlawai. Some were able to master the ability to utilize organic technologies within their consciousness and yet, they have been rare indeed. On Earth, they have been seen as Ascended Masters, gods, and avatars depending on the culture and timeframe. The technologies and practices of the Hindu yogis have come close to remembering the potential that the Hōlawai are accustomed to. Yet, they have only skimmed the surface of how to truly implement them. It has remained contained to small numbers and, therefore, has yet to be integrated into the collective technologies in a way that serves both Beauty and function anywhere close to what is possible.

The current density within human consciousness made it a challenging and delicate mission to Awaken Beki in just the perfect way so that she could bring this frequency of Hōlawai into her unique gifts/hamanaku. Each being holds the blueprint for their soul's purpose within a particular embodiment. It is important to honor this when infusing any influence into another self so that it will enhance the original blueprint rather than interfere. It must align with both the human soul and the Higher Self/OverSoul. Therefore, while Namundhi could assist her as a Guide, it was Shahalaku who must infuse the unique frequencies of Awakening that align with their shared Higher Self. The innate wisdom of their shared Soul would know precisely what activations of ReMembering would be most beneficial and when the timing would be best for the desired results.

The first point of influence was when the entity known as Beki was still crawling, and her consciousness was still new to the dimension of separation and polarity. The thought was introduced into her young, inquisitive mind, "Would this world exist if I were not in it?" This simple yet profound thought marked the beginning of a philosophical quest for a deeper, esoteric understanding of life in which she reached beyond the world of matter and the ordinary consciousness of her time. Her father intuitively recognized her "non-conforming" nature with a pang of pride for her inquisitiveness and assertion to think for herself. She had chosen the perfect parental figures to cultivate her unique ways of seeing and navigating the human world.

Her father was a professor of social ethics, a human rights activist, and a great lover of art and beauty. Her mother was an artist and art teacher who facilitated a profound Awakening which was instrumental in attuning Beki to her Soul. This occurred one fateful day when she urged Beki to sit in meditation before beginning to paint and then to focus purely on the creation process, releasing all expectations or attachments to the end product.

This was not a usual form of learning at that time, as most humans focused primarily on an outcome and achieving the end goal, which usurped their true source of creative power. Beki's mother had been her art teacher in high school, and her attempts to get her to paint without using a reference to copy were always met with great resistance. Beki had become attached to the approval she received from her art, and subconsciously, she feared diverging from this safe and more realistic approach to painting. Her mother sensed this was limiting her creativity and continued encouraging her. On this particular day, she was able to get Beki to acquiesce when she offered the caveat that she would not have to show the painting to her or anyone else. She left her alone in the apartment to be free to create without any outer gaze.

This destined event happened when Beki was seventeen years old which was considered around the age of adulthood in her country at the time. Namundhi and Shahalaku agreed this would be a good time to activate this potent Awakening to align her hamanaku with her soul's purpose. The entity that served as her mother was aligned to this activation and, at a Soul level, joyfully agreed to participate in this initiation.

In this ecstatic moment of creation, Beki made conscious contact with her Soul/OverSoul, and her hamanaku was activated in complete alignment with her Divine Blueprint. Not only did Beki feel the shackles of her need for approval fall away, but she could also feel the power of her True Voice unleashed — a voice that spoke boldly with the vibrations of color and shapes, creating powerful movements of energy. She was changed forever. Her art would become a path of Awakening to her Divine Self and carry the frequency for this Soul-alignment from this point forward.

It was quite a moment of celebration for the Hōwaka-heh women in Hōlawai'kiki! They were overjoyed that Beki chose to reclaim connection with her Soul and take the path of Awakening. It was a fork in her road in which she had a distinct choice — the journey of Awakening or the path of continued amnesia. All other choices that lay ahead on her path were at that moment altered to reflect the choice to Awaken. There had been a series of smaller activations of Hōlawai frequencies of Oneness prior to this moment to inspire this choice, but this was the real turning point that assured Namundhi and Shahala that Beki was in alignment with the frequencies they already embodied themselves. They knew their efforts to infuse their love and support would bear great fruits as she continued this journey.

FOURTEEN

The Window of Opportunity

Wa'kamema Hah'laqua
Kinyah kinyah
Shahala koko hah'nah tatata taa

From this point forward, the holy women were able to infuse Beki's consciousness with impulses that came in many creative forms. Shahalaku would consult her Soul, who was the source of Beki's guidance as well, for ways to activate her Awakening. Then and now Namundhi assisted her with a plan of action. It was a wonderful exploration for them both, all within the Hah'laqua/the Eternal Moment of Now, beyond time. Intuitively and with great precision, they sent impulses into the entire life of Beki up to the moment in which Namundhi's disembodied soul was ReMembered by Beki with the aid of the mystic medium.

In the meantime, they continued to enjoy life in the beautiful Land of Waterfalls. Shahalaku found a great appreciation for the new experiences that Beki inspired, allowing her to ReMember more of herself. The aching desire to be able to bear and birth children was assuaged as she tuned into Beki's experiences of becoming a mother to her three beautiful sons. While the concept of mothering in her world was very different from the world of the Hōlawai, she was able to feel the distinct quality of love engendered through these relationships along with the contrasting agony Beki felt as she sought to deal with the struggles and adversities that her sons would endure.

The attachment to her sons' emotional and physical well-being caused Beki unnecessary suffering. If only she could ReMember the Truth of their Wholeness as Divine Eternal Beings, perhaps she would not be so affected by their contractions — the difficult emotions and conditions that they chose for their evolution and growth before incarnating. While she attempted to infuse this wisdom into Beki frequently, she could feel the overwhelming waves of emotions that would push back her gifts of ReMembering. Shahala needed to wait until a moment of ripeness to use this powerful life force of mother-love to initiate a new level of Oneness Consciousness for Beki to embody. This was essential for Beki to be able to fulfill her hamanaku as an agent of Awakening during this great, tumultuous time of transformation on Earth.

Despite the resistance Shahalaku observed from Beki's stubborn and strange propensity to constantly worry and fret over the well-being of her children, Shahala relished the mothering experience that she was able to sense from her own perspective. Shahala loved Beki's sons and felt the familiar knowing of their souls as she witnessed the beauty of their self-expression. These deeply wise beings were well suited for the parents who were so devoted to them, each in their own unique way.

Their father was what one may call the "rock" of the family. He grounded them all in the Earth-frequency and tended to the human needs in ways that made them all feel safe and loved. In this way, he was a great source of inspiration for the hamanaku of each family member to become recognized and fostered. It made life in this strange world more bearable for Beki to be loved by such a man. His devotion to her and their sons made Shahalaku feel warm and grateful for his commitment to this part of her own Soul that Beki was. She immediately fell in love with them all as she observed their evolution.

Beki embodied the mother/wa'kamema energy with much grace most of the time; with occasional dramatic moments of exasperation when she became consumed by worry, her need to control, or her longing for freedom from this responsibility. Beki recognized that the role of human mother was a part of her Awakening journey and sought to find balance and connection to her divine, unlimited nature without losing herself in the intensity of mothering. She brought her own potent energy to the experiences of the family by modeling this journey of Awakening and holding a container for her sons to explore their own souls' paths.

Beki's sons offered catalytic energies for her evolution. Each son embodied a different quality within himself and in his life choices that would stimulate her self-contemplation and reclamation of her inner power. Of course, this is true of all core relationships across all time and space. It is a symbiotic exchange that brings forth opportunities for growth. When one chooses to expand and evolve because of challenging dynamics in relationships and life experiences, they create a potent frequency for the Whole to experience the fruits of this intention.

For Shahalaku, it was a delicious dance to observe. It inspired her in certain explorations of her own relationships within her unique dimension of reality. For one thing, it seemed to soothe her aching desire to be a mother herself. She was able to live vicariously through this other self, who was embodied as Beki, and sense the fullness of mothering in this way. She also was able to truly embrace the power of her special gifts and her chosen life path with new vigor and appreciation. She was gaining a new perspective that was greatly helpful in the evolution of her hamanaku. This creative journey of assisting Beki in her Awakening was a catalyst for her own development and expansion.

For instance, Shahalaku had the opportunity to experience the exciting new technology that her community had co-created, which she had not yet needed until now — the Quantum Chamber of Timelessness for traveling to other dimensions. This would enable her to connect with Beki more directly.

The chamber consisted of crystal walls and was carved and embedded into the side of the mountain that was home to the Waterfall of Unlimited Possibility. The synergistic frequencies of the water/iōwai from a specific sacred Waterfall, the essences of flowers and plants within the water, and the crystalline energy from the chamber, created a potent environment for time travel. The iōwai/water was channeled in such a way as to encase the outside of the crystalline walls, infusing the frequencies of Infinite Possibility Possibility into the chamber. Specific stones, crystals, light codes within vacillating color spectrums, sound frequencies, and geometric equations were all precisely synchronized to initiate teleportation to any chosen space or time. This was a magnificently elegant system that was enhanced by the intention of the user who would bring their signature frequency to the process by chanting distinct tones to indicate their particular organic essence. This was an essential component of this technology: to utilize the frequencies of both matter and spirit to ensure a positive outcome when traversing time and space.

Shahalaku and Namundhi were assessing how best to use this function to support Beki in her Awakening. They knew how delicate and precise this visitation must be and how critical it was that Beki was ready. The approach used to interject the presence of Shahalaku into her consciousness was key. As mentioned before, premature influence could cause confusion or discomfort to Beki's mind and body. They desired to be as gentle as possible and at the same time deliver the most potent frequency of Oneness and Wholeness into Beki's consciousness.

The day came when they felt they had deciphered a wonderful window of opportunity. It was when Shahalaku recognized the eldest son of Beki as the same Soul embodied as the Emperor's son from her life as a Portuguese Priest. As she marveled at this realization, she could feel an emotional pull from Beki, who was worrying about this same son whose potent bond traversed time and space. As the power of her mother-love equaled her painful attachment to the need for his well-being, Beki's sense of despair and hopelessness crescendoed. While this pattern had surfaced before, Shahalaku knew that a certain quality of resonance was needed for her to plunge into Beki's reality. The opportunity revealed itself when she felt a release of resistance, a complete surrender of control. At this moment Beki submitted to the Light. For she had no other choice.

FIFTEEN

Eagle Medicine and Merging

Hee'ti kah'waha
Hee'ti kah'waha
Doosh'dahah Aho

Early one fateful morning, Beki was walking through a beautiful, wooded park, close to her home, along the lush, golden-green marsh common to the Lowcountry of South Carolina. She was feeling a foreboding sense of despair and hopelessness as she pined helplessly over her eldest son flailing through the treacherous terrain of adolescence. She ached to do the right thing, to fix his problems, to control the conditions of his life. In her mind, she would berate herself, not to mention her son and her husband, with thoughts and stories that tortured her. Nobody was doing this life right and it all felt unbearably unmanageable. That morning, something extraordinary happened.

She felt herself release control.

Involuntarily, she surrendered...fully.

Was it just a moment? A nanosecond? Was it the whole walk through the sheltered path of beauty? Whatever it was, Shahalaku saw this as the moment that she would be able to effortlessly stretch out of no-time into the world of Beki. She stood in readiness in the crystal Quantum Chamber of Timelessness and began the sacred chants with stones in hand to amplify the frequencies of Oneness and Unconditional Love from her own world. Namundhi stood nearby, outside the chamber, chanting prayers and holding sacred space for the magical unfolding to occur. There were other Hōwaka-heh present to anchor certain frequencies to assure that Shahalaku would return safely after her mission was complete.

It was an exhilarating moment for both Shahalaku and Beki when the two merged in the liminal space between worlds. A warm, bright light burst through the darkness of despair and amnesia. Instantly Beki was AWAKE!

Just prior to that moment, Beki had lifted her head, beseeching the Divine Realm she so loved, calling out with exasperation, "God, please, give me a sign." At this moment, she yearned for something concrete to let her know she was not alone and that her son was not alone. She needed a little magic to help her continue. Within seconds of her plea, as she walked towards the dock on the wooden boardwalk, she felt and heard the swoosh of a big bird fly overhead. A beautiful bald eagle glided and landed right in front of her on a lamppost! She froze in awe. Her tears dried instantly, and she searched her surroundings to see if there was anyone else around to witness this unusual and majestic sight.

No one.

This was the moment Shahalaku swooped in and merged her consciousness with Beki's. The two became one. The One, that was many, felt the merging as well — for an instant, in the Hah'laqua/the Eternal Moment of Now, their OverSoul and the two embodied souls reveled in the power and sweetness of this homecoming. It was extraordinary.

For Shahalaku, it was a mix of sensations that she found fascinating. While the body and energy field of Beki was much smaller than hers, it was infinitely heavier and denser. She could immediately sense the pull of gravity in this place in a way that made the body feel like lead in comparison to her own world. As she took a deep breath, she observed how Beki's breath was short and constricted, with small channels for the air to enter. Yet, at the same time, she marveled at the pungent aroma of the marsh and the spring air which was reminiscent of the wet air of her beloved home. The scent of the salty sea was distinctly different from the moist fragrance of the flower-infused waterfalls in the mountains. Shahalaku quite liked it. The temperature felt both warm and cool with the morning dew visibly glistening on the surrounding plant life.

She curiously observed the inner and outer terrain that she had just entered. The eagle was truly magnificent! What a wonderful symbol that Beki's Life Guides (the Spirit Guides who are with you throughout a lifetime) chose to send her when she requested, with such sincerity, a sign from God that she was not alone. She could feel the significance of this ancient symbol that was iconic in the indigenous shamanic traditions in the early Americas, the landmass to which Beki belonged at this time.

These shamans would speak of Eagle medicine as that which Awakens you from the nightmare of your unconscious creations so that you can dream a new world consciously and with intention. This is specifically what Shahalaku initiated in the communal Creation Ceremonies when they brought together the collective imagination aligned with Soul Memory for the purpose of conscious, intentional creation. Eagle medicine allows you to see from the broad view, the birds-eye view, which soars above the minute details of life.

This is the view of the Infinite Soul Self that the Hōlawai tap into during their ceremonies. For them, the eagle's perspective symbolizes that of the Soul that guides the embodied human soul. The energy of this beautiful bird infused Beki with the essence of this new perspective along with the power and strength it possessed. Shahalaku could feel the medicine of the Eagle working synergistically with her loving intention to Awaken her beloved iōwayah'ho-kiki /soul-kin. She could feel the power of these collaborating forces activating this Memory within Beki.

As Shahalaku contemplated the brilliant choice for Beki's Spirit Guides to activate the Eagle medicine in this potent way, she observed the beauty of the marsh surrounding them— a lush shade of green, reminiscent of burgeoning new life, met the clear blue of a vast open sky. There was something settling and peaceful about this view of Earth. Yet, the heaviness and ache within the mind and emotions of Beki were quite a contrast to the outer vision of peace. Shahalaku felt the clutter of her thoughts. It was no wonder she was feeling so much pain. There was no space to allow Love to communicate Its clear, wise knowing. Her mind was filled with fear and worrisome thoughts that were full of static, obscuring the clear signal of her own Soul.

This sensation was so foreign to Shahalaku that she needed to activate her faculties of toko-magua/focused attention to make sure she did not become lost in these discordant thoughts and fall under the spell of amnesia, forgetting why she came in the first place. It was imperative that she maintain her distinct frequency and not meld completely with Beki's current state of mind. All this observation happened within a moment in Beki's time, while in no-time it could have seemed much longer. The Hōlawai naturally stretched and condensed "time" based on their desired experience and intentions.

Shahalaku began to immediately direct her energy with the distinct and powerful essence of Unconditional Love into the mind of Beki. She encouraged all the cluttered and painful thoughts to arise to the surface of the mind, and then she bathed each thought with this Divine frequency of Pure Love. Like rapid fire, the thoughts were transmuted and transformed into a higher Truth of profound wisdom. The Knowing that was buried in Beki, by these conditioned thoughts and beliefs, emerged and she was able to sense a new mind, a new perspective.

As Beki stood on the wooden dock, absorbing the magnificence of this great bird, she simultaneously felt a different frequency trickle into her being. It was a lightness that felt foreign yet familiar all at once. It was a spaciousness that filled her body and mind — an indescribable peace. Her body was being caressed with waves of sweet, tingling energy causing her skin to become covered in goosebumps. She assumed it this was inspired by the magical sight of the Bald Eagle as a stunning recognition of her request for a sign. A profound feeling of gratitude and awe broke through the dense state of fear and despair that had consumed her only seconds before. Of course, she was unaware of Shahalaku. She would not consciously be aware of her existence for many years. Yet, she could feel her. That was undeniable.

She noticed the thoughts that had been plaguing her begin to arise and fall away almost immediately. The story playing out in her mind was being revealed as false, and she could viscerally sense the deconstruction of these nagging mental constructs. In their place arose a spacious energy of Pure Love.

Throughout the following days, she would feel a distinct difference in her thinking. It was not as though there were no thoughts. Rather, the thoughts felt peaceful and wise and aligned to this frequency of Unconditional Love. It made her aware of how conditional her love had been for her children and everyone, particularly for this beloved son who frequently triggered her worry during this time of his life. She so desperately wanted him to be healthy and happy and safe — conditions she felt were necessary for her to stay connected to the frequency of Love.

This was not Love at all, she realized. Yet it is the way most humans love. It is this human concept of love that causes so much suffering for so many mothers *and* fathers. It is a love bound to fear, worry, and control, which in truth, is not Love at all, but a shadow version of It. This is what the divided mind does. It was the infusion of Unconditional Love born of the Truth of Oneness, undivided and Whole, that allowed Beki to experience a new state of Being.

Shahalaku had witnessed this as she was observing the life of Beki after she and Namundhi decided to intercede to offer their gifts to help Beki evolve her own hamanaku of healing to assist others in their Awakening journey. She felt the strangeness of this mother-love of Beki's time which was both intoxicating and disconcerting to her all at once. It made her appreciate the way the Hōlawai experienced motherhood from the perspective of Oneness, Creation, and Unconditional Love.

The wa'kamema/mama never felt burdened by their role as mother since the entire community parented the children. Moreover, the conditions for worry were simply not a part of their world. Shahalaku realized how incredibly challenging it must be to be wa'kamema in a world such as this one. She felt a deep sense of compassion and admiration for the souls who entered such a conditional reality where the majority of beings did not realize that they were the creators of the world that they often felt helplessly victims of.

Beki marinated in the utterly blissful sense of relief as she integrated the pure presence and Love of Shahalaku, who reflected Divine Love so clearly. After all, Shahala had practiced her devotion to the Loving Self, her Soul Essence, from the moment of her birth.

As Beki continued her day, the profound shift in her consciousness became more and more undeniable. While she still encountered the same disturbing, unwanted conditions in her personal world, she could not even pretend to be upset by them. Her perspective was completely transformed. She was seeing through the clear lens that Shahalaku was presenting with her powerful Loving presence. It was as though she had been looking through a pair of glasses that were not only filthy with dirt and smudges, but they were not even *her* prescription, creating further distortion. She had inherited them from generations of human beings who bore their particular misunderstandings, misperceptions, and misidentifications.

Shahalaku's influence offered a clear window of perception that was initiating a permanent, visceral shift in consciousness. Beki's vision was infused with the perspective of Shahalaku while they were merged, which added its own unique and potent frequency of Awakened Mind. This aspect of the infusion would be temporary, of course, for Shahalaku had time-traveled into this world and would need to return when the time was right. For Beki, to be merged with Shahalaku was so profoundly different from her normal state of mind, that she immediately knew she was experiencing what only the legendary masters known on Earth have achieved. It was utter liberation.

As Beki reconnected with her family, her husband, and most significantly, her eldest son, she noticed the extreme difference in how she felt and behaved with them before the Awakening. Without the burden of worry and the need to control, nor the obsession with the painful past and future fears, she was able to focus fully on the sweetness of the present moment. It allowed her to experience an extraordinary sense of intimacy and presence she had never known was possible. She easily leaned into the *apparent* suffering of her son with a pure and Unconditional Love that amazed her. She felt a liberating sense of non-attachment to anything which, paradoxically, allowed her to feel more connected than ever!

It turns out that the ancient yogic practice of detachment allows for a deeper intimacy with all of Life. It is the attachments that clutter the mind and fog up our screen of perception. This keeps us from being fully present in the Eternal Now, which is when and where all life is happening. All that is real, is now. So, when the mind is clear of past and future, the possibility for intimacy, connection, and presence emerges naturally.

Beki was amazed at the compassion that washed over her for herself, for her son, and for her husband, who too had been navigating the mind-field of parenting with the futile grasping for control of the uncontrollable child. While they had struggled to find the best approach, it had put a strain on their relationship. In this Awakened state of presence, all of this melted away, and she fell in love with her beloved husband all over again. She did not need him to agree with her or for her to agree with him. She needed nothing from him. This gave her the space to *see* him more fully. His beauty, love, and commitment to her and their boys was undeniable. As she was bathed in this Pure Frequency of Love of her True Self, she could only see and feel Love no matter the condition. Her heart was on fire and her whole being was at peace.

This Awakened state of Being lasted a full week of blissful reunion with her True nature. Slowly, Beki felt the intensity of this non-ordinary state, at least for her world, fade away. Yet she was not dismayed or saddened by this, but rather full of gratitude to have been able to experience an extended period in which she was fully Awake. She now knew what was possible for her and all of humanity. She sensed the organic, innate technology for Awakening within her, and knew that she would always have this Knowing to guide her, and eventually others, to this promised land of our True Home.

SIXTEEN

Shahalaku Returns Home

Wah'halama Toka Maya
Xlhanima Xlhanima Xlhanima

Shahalaku was deeply moved by the effects of her offering as she experienced the shift in Beki's consciousness while she was merged with her. She could feel her heart and body embrace her son amid his stormy emotional terrain when she usually would have become consumed by the ache of worry. She knew that she could not stay with Beki, or she would lose her distinct expression and the life she loved. So, when she felt that she had effectively anchored this memory of True Love into Beki's consciousness, Shahalaku indicated to Namundhi, through her telepathic faculties, that she was ready to return. Of course, understand that while the melding of souls lasted only moments in the dimension of no time, for Beki it seemed like a whole week.

This stretching and condensing of time is critical to the function of interdimensional travel. This capacity within the technology in the world of Hōlawai'kiki is a natural part of how they experience reality. First, they must conceive the idea born of desire, which often occurs when communing with Soul Memory either in Collective Ceremony or in a solo communion with Soul Self. Then the ability to receive the wisdom and knowledge necessary to create technologies such as the Quantum Chamber of Timelessness came very naturally to them. It must be understood that without Sacred Wisdom, this knowledge would not be accessible. Wisdom was valued over knowledge for this reason.

Not only do the Hōlawai resource their own Wah'halama/Soul Memory for manifesting new Creation, but they also communicate directly with the animal kingdom, in Sacred Ceremony, to attune their Collective Vision/Toka-Maya with the beloved beasts of their land. This process supports the Hōlawai in creating and utilizing this and other innovative and powerful technologies, in a way that is harmonious and beneficial for all, including the natural world around them.

Within moments of indicating her desire to return home, Shahalaku felt reconnected to her own body. It felt so weightless and full of light that she was amazed at the sensation of returning home. Without such contrasting realities in her world, it was an unusual and sumptuous sensation to feel the radiance and power of her body with such intensity. It would be inaccurate to say that she took it for granted. She felt a profound appreciation for the beauty of her Being and existence. However, it indeed was a unique and compelling experience to feel the power of returning. It helped her to understand why so many souls choose to embody in the denser planes of Earth. It enabled her to appreciate Beki's choice. It gave her a feeling of reverence for the courage of the soul of Beki and others to intentionally choose such repressive conditions so that they could offer their Light to lift the veil of forgetfulness. Beki's timeline was particularly potent because of the Awakening revolution gradually taking hold within human consciousness.

As Shahalaku had become aware of Beki and this period within human history, she was able to see that in the formless dimension, countless souls were clamoring to go to the Earth during this transitional time so they could assist in elevating the consciousness of humanity. It was known throughout the Universe that life on Earth was poised for a potential mass extinction event. These souls entered this physical plane with extraordinary enthusiasm and optimism that they would be able to help Awaken enough of humanity so that they might remember that they had a *choice* to alter course. However, once in the world of form, so many souls become lost in the amnesia with which they agreed to cloak themselves in order to enter such density and polarity. Otherwise, their undivided frequency could not sustain itself within the human body of this time. Awakening, for the most part, must be gradual, or the soul would simply choose to ascend out of the conditions that felt so oppressive and constrictive to its natural Essence.

That is why Beki was not yet ready to stay fully Awakened. She needed to assimilate the new frequencies and walk the path of freedom. Then, she would have specific tools native to the people of that time that she could use to support them in their Awakening, too. Her journey and her commitment to self-inquiry were a rich training ground where she would accumulate the knowledge and wisdom to offer her gifts.

This Awakening facilitated by Shahalaku, in alignment with her Life Guides, was a significant activator for Beki's gift as a healer. It Awakened her hamanaku. Although she had spent a lifetime cultivating her connection to the Divine and developing her art forms of painting and writing, both of which would play a key role in her offerings, she did not know the direction it would take for several more years. However, now the trajectory of her path was assured.

SEVENTEEN

Animal Attunement Ceremony

Hōwaka-heh tah'nani-kiki
mallee honi makawah'ha
Hōlimama Fafui

After her intriguing adventure with Beki, Shahalaku could not stop thinking about how beautifully the Eagle medicine had activated this powerful opportunity for Awakening. She marveled at how indigenous wisdom was still assisting humanity's evolution, even in this time when amnesia was so prevalent. She was fascinated by how her world overlapped with Beki's. As one of the twelve Hōwaka who presided over their village, she was very much attuned to the power of animal medicine and the gift they offer to the balance and harmony of the Whole.

Shahalaku was in awe at how the Quantum Chamber of Timelessness allowed for this profound interaction between her and her iōwayah'ho-kiki in another dimension. She remembered when this Creative Vision of the Quantum Chamber was first conceived as she was one of the Hōwaka who facilitated the Creation Ceremony/Hōlimama Fafui. It was exhilarating to experience the emergence of this Toka-Maya/Collective Vision. This technology would unveil infinite worlds to explore – a desire that was at the heart of the Vision.

The Animal Attunement Ceremony, which must follow each Hōlimama Fafui, is an exquisite experience in and of itself. Each Hōwaka is responsible for communing with their correlating animal-kin, who presides over an aspect of the animal kingdom and the land they steward. As Shahala contemplated the majestic eagle that soared into Beki's world, she felt her heart swell with love as her memory transported her to a divine communion with her animal-kin during one of the Attunement Ceremonies not long ago…

Shahalaku sat in the middle of a circle of twelve polished, oval stones about six feet tall lining the circumference. Each had a beautiful design carved into them, embedded with crystals of many colors. They were organic yet resplendently ornate at the same time. She sat cross-legged on the ground in an inner circle covered with soft moss scented with ceremonial oils, poised to call forth her animal-kin to align the Toka-Maya with the animal kingdom of the Hōlawai'kiki. Radiating from this inner circle were twelve spoke-like linear paver stones that met the large rocks. The space between each spoke was like a soft green carpet of mossy grass filled with flowers in perpetual bloom.

Shahalaku was adorned in her favorite colorful ceremonial garment. Her head was wrapped in an orange and green turban. She wore a large pendant necklace that sat directly over her throat, made of petrified wood covered with gold – a symbol of the Earth's gift of majesty. Her elegant and slender hands held a large golden goblet filled with nectar from the fruit of a rare tree that grows on top of the mountain that is home to the Waterfall of Magic and Mysteries. This nectar is reserved for the Hōwaka-heh/Priest/esses, which they only use for the solo ceremonies specifically to birth the Toka-Maya/Collective Vision already conceived during the Hōlimama-Fafui/Creation Ceremony.

As stated earlier, it is imperative that after every Creation Ceremony, each of the twelve Hōwaka-heh takes turns bringing the Toka-Maya into resonance with all the land's inhabitants through communion with the animal kingdom. The harmonic manifestation of the Vision must come into attunement with the Whole to benefit all.

During the Attunement Ceremony, each linear paver, connected to a large, vertical stone, becomes activated by the intention of the Hōwaka-heh. A frequency of love, gratitude, and respect initiates a vibration that travels through the paver, beckoning the presence of the specific animal-kin of the presiding Hōwaka. Then, the crystals within the stone become infused with the Toka-Maya held by the intention and frequency of the Hōwaka in Ceremony. With an electric-like charge, the information is conveyed to this kingdom of the wild in a way that the animal can fully understand. This Ceremony is telepathically initiated by the Hōwaka. It is how they maintain harmony between the Vision of the people and the environment in which they inhabit.

Shahalaku felt a ripple of excitement anticipating the sacred meeting with her tah'nani-kiki. She lifted the golden goblet to her lips, receiving the coveted nectar into her mouth. She immediately felt the powerful shift in perception, enabling her to communicate clearly with her animal-kin. As she commenced a holy chant, her body quickly began to tingle with the unique frequencies of her beloved cat. The majestic leopard of unparalleled grace and beauty emerged from behind the fifth stone, seemingly out of nowhere. He glided toward her through the sacred space and greeted her where she sat. She reached out to caress his silky, smooth fur as he wrapped around her slender, tall frame. The kinship between them was undeniable. After some time of being enraptured by this reunion, she focused on the Toka-Maya to offer the transmission to her tah'nani-kiki.

This stunningly majestic animal locked his piercing gaze with hers for what felt like an eternity. Their mutual love and respect for each other was extraordinary, giving off a distinctly sweet scent. As they held this trance of transmission, a new chant emerged from the Priestess's body. The leopard, in unison, vibrated a powerful, audible chant that seemed to shake the massive stones surrounding this ceremonial dance of energy. Shahala could sense her body lifting from the ground as the vibration of the meeting kingdoms accelerated with the pure intent of harmonic creation.

Time stood still, as it tends to in the beautiful land of Hōlawai'kiki. There was a definite and distinct sense of realignment of the reality they shared. The birthing was underway. The agreement was sealed with this honored meeting. Soon, Shahala felt her beloved tah'nani-kiki begin to gently bow in recognition of this sacred attunement. They were now in alignment with the Toka-Maya and would honor the continued unfolding of its manifestation. With reverence, she lowered her head, tears rolling down her face, her heart overflowing with love and gratitude for this union. She reached out again to touch the purring heart of her kin, feeling the synchronization of the rhythm that gave them life. Then he turned and walked the circle, marking each stone with his scent and intent, disappearing behind the fifth rock. The rock lit up and emanated the colors of the crystals into the dark sky. This sealed the energetic agreement with the frequency of the land and animals that her tah'nani-kiki presided over.

This Ceremony would be repeated with each of the other Hōwaka and their respective tah'nani-kiki. Each would bring their distinct frequency, aroma, and essence to the process. Once the twelfth stone was brought into Ceremony, the manifestation would be complete, and the beings of the land would all delight in the effortless unfolding and fruition of their Vision. This is one of the magical ceremonies of this world that is created purely through their intention, imagination, love, and Soul-knowing. It is simple, creative, and sustainable. It honors the individual and the All in a way that creates harmony, abundance, peace, and profound beauty.

While Shahala loved the world she co-created with the magic and wonder that seemed to unfold daily within this space, she found herself appreciating more and more the richness of the world of her iōwayah'ho-kiki/soul-kin, Beki, who inhabited a land and dimension so different from hers. She was intrigued by the strange beauty that she witnessed through her, even though it was so intensely dense and filled with daily inner and outer conflicts. She noticed an extraordinary resilience and creativity born from these struggles. The insights and self-awareness emerging in Beki's consciousness were unending. The pain seemed to be consistently matched by a powerful insight and an Awakening of consciousness happening within the container of linear time.

Yet, Shahalaku experienced life in "no time," so feelings and conditions were fully felt and then shifted quickly. She observed that for those in Beki's world, time became a source of so much of their suffering, aggravated by self-doubt and a lack of trust or faith in life. It took great concentration and love to live in this time. Her intrigue and respect for those exploring this world inspired her to continue to bring her toko-magua to this part of herself, her iōwayah'ho-kiki, to offer her support.

EIGHTEEN

Pandemic Chaos

Ha hakaka ha hakaka
Walka'wah hata
Haa haa haa

It was the Spring of 2022, two years after our world was told by the leaders across the lands that there was a deadly virus sweeping across the human populations. They were instructed to stay home, keep a distance from other humans, wash their hands incessantly to avoid contracting this disease, and wear a mask while in public, along with many other measures. As the governments announced this pandemic, they enforced strict lockdowns in cities and towns where they were able to broadcast their messaging far and near.

The last two years of chaos initiated a great Awakening that had been brewing for some time, as the people of Earth decided what they believed or didn't believe and how they would navigate the psychic warfare that ensued. The eons of separation consciousness and the war mentality, perpetuated by the cycle of victim-villain-savior triangulation, came to a head.

After the initial few months of the lockdowns, there was a distinct splitting of ways in which this calamity would be perceived. It was a fascinating drama to witness from the world of Shahalaku. For the Hōlawai, not only are all perspectives allowed, but they are also celebrated as an essential aspect of the Whole. They consider diversity, in all ways, as a great strength that is both natural and necessary. Every person has a unique way of being and perceiving, offering the community extraordinary riches and infinite wisdom. This ensures the evolution and harmony of the Whole.

Consider the analogy of the puzzle, with each piece being completely unique and each person representing one piece of the Whole. For all parts to experience the Whole, each individual piece must be their authentic, unique self to fit into the distinct space they belong to, completing the Whole. Therefore, everyone benefits from the diversity of shape and color of each puzzle piece. If one piece feels it should be like another and tries to alter its true nature, it would become a missing piece since it would no longer fit into the space that was perfect for it.

Shahala was fascinated at how the humans seemed blind to this simple wisdom. They often insisted that others agree and follow their belief systems. This was mind-bending to her. As she observed this dynamic within Beki's world, she watched how the mounting pressure to conform and follow a homogeneous perspective was causing more and more disharmony in a world already torn apart. This went against everything true for the Hōlawai and negated the ability to follow one's innate guidance from the Higher Self. It was causing great conflict and strife among not only ideologies of governmental parties, religious sectors, and communities, but it seemed to infiltrate the very fabric of family units. This dividing of loved ones, with such authoritarian measures, devastated the families, organizations, businesses, and individuals who became plagued with self-doubt and feelings of fear of the very people they loved most. As the inner wars, festering in the minds of individuals, raged unchecked, the conditions for the outer wars became inevitable.

The verbal, emotional, physical, political, social, and racial violence was becoming more and more amplified. It seemed that *everything* could be a trigger. The pandemic became fertile ground for the polarizations of sides to become more extreme. Amid all this chaos, Shahalaku and Namundhi recognized this was also a ripe time for transformation. There was indeed a great Awakening underway. The systems that had long been respected were crumbling in the eyes of the people. Who or what could they trust? While this could feel devastating and terrifying to many, from a broader perspective, it was necessary for the people to realize that they must take back their power. Once they reclaimed their sovereignty as divine, creative beings, they could start molding their world as they chose without feeling a victim of the systems outside their control. As long as they were entangled in the triangulation of victimhood, victory would elude them.

The Hōwaka-heh observed that if they engaged in this disempowering dynamic of *victim-villain-savior,* they would be trapped in this illusory construct of victimhood, believing they were not participating in creating their own life experience. In Hōlawai'kiki, there was never anyone to save. For what or whom would they save themselves from? Therefore, no one was perceived as a victim, and the idea of a villain was inconceivable. They understand that they create their own reality and that all beings are a part of the Whole. Creating villains would inflict pain on themselves. With their innate understanding of Oneness, harming or banishing any piece of the Whole/puzzle would be self-destructive.

Namundhi and Shahala also understood that within the dimension of time and space that Beki was experiencing, humanity had chosen to explore a very different reality that reflected the story of separation, polarity, and duality. From their perspective they observed the outcomes of these unconscious creations. Yet, they assumed that surely, if they were not beholden to the function of amnesia, they would not choose thoughts, beliefs, or actions that would cause such unthinkable conditions as starvation, war, disease, and the most egregious acts of violence.

For Shahalaku, one of the most devastating outcomes of such separation consciousness and extreme amnesia was the epidemic of 'suicide.' During the pandemic, this phenomenon rose significantly. The feeling of disconnection and isolation was already rampant. Still, when populations were told to literally isolate themselves from others to be safe from the virus and keep their loved ones safe, it sent a wave of fear through humanity. The desperation became too unbearable for many.

It was utterly inconceivable to the Hōlawai to cause the unwanted death of another being, let alone take their own life out of desperation, seeking relief. There was no justification within their world to do such a thing, for they would not choose to destroy what they had chosen to create. They also understood death as a glorious transition; in their world, it was *chosen,* not as an escape from life but as a way to continue life in a new way. Killing another to punish or enact revenge was unimaginable. For '*death*' was a sacred transition deeply honored and revered in Hōlawai'kiki. She and her fellow Hōwaka loved to facilitate ceremonies to support the beings who were initiating their ascension into their next life adventure. It made her so sad to think of all these beautiful souls who were experiencing disease, despair, and disillusionment as a part of the way they transitioned out of this physical plane. Not only was it an abysmal process for the one "dying," but it caused great suffering and confusion for those "left behind."

Shahala was beginning to sense that this alien approach to death and life was a phenomenon of amnesia. She contemplated this dilemma simultaneously with her soul-kin, who was also trying to make sense of the world she inhabited. Unknowingly, Beki could feel the thoughts of Shahalaku tickle her mind infusing the perspective from another dimension of another self who effortlessly embodied Oneness.

Shahala pondered: *If you know you are the creator of your reality, and your whole community understands this, creating experiences you prefer and that benefit the Whole is a joyous adventure. It is a life of unlimited creation and self-expression. Yet, if you have forgotten that you are the creator, you may sink into fear, control, and violence because you are reacting to the conditions of the world as though you were a victim of it. When this happens, people* **unconsciously** *create their life experiences, many of which they would never have chosen if they were aware. As they absorb the beliefs from the collective while under the trance of amnesia, rather than receiving guidance directly from their own Soul, they seem to create their reality by default rather than intention. Many of these beliefs* *are not only undesired by the one inheriting them but also by those who pass them down. They just don't realize that they have a choice. As they practice these beliefs they are eventually perceived as "truths" with irrefutable and empirical evidence reflecting this reality. However, this reflection is not evidence of truth. Rather, it is the faithful function of the Universe responding to the focused attention/toko-magua given to staunchly held beliefs. The Hōlawai understand how powerful our toko-magua is in creating reality. Therefore, we are very intentional about choosing wisely where we place our attention.*

Of course, this world held its own distinct adventure, offering its inhabitants extraordinary challenges to navigate. Shahalaku understood that at the Soul level, everyone in all times and dimensions chooses the life and world they embody, each with unique intentions and desires for the ultimate purpose of experiencing, evolving, and expanding.

Since Beki had chosen to come to Earth during this time in history, she understood the challenges she would face *before* incarnation. She and her Spirit Guides designed a Divine Blueprint to support her in creating the desired experience so that the intense terrain of amnesia would not completely prevent her from finding her way. Many signposts were put in place that would guide her. Her personality contained distinct traits that would cause her to gravitate toward certain information that would support her Awakening. Awakening to the Divine Truth of Oneness and Unconditional Love was what Beki desired to experience more than anything. This yearning gave rise to her desire to be a catalyst for the Awakening of others. She wanted to know what it was like to forget to ReMember. She had come to the right time and space to enable such an experience.

One quality of her personality that helped serve this desire was her tendency to question the status quo. She did not automatically believe those in authority positions, whether a schoolteacher, a medical doctor, a politician, or a religious leader. She naturally did not simply conform to the typical path people were expected to take. This non-conforming nature revealed itself in many ways throughout her life, with the family and parents she chose and distinct events in her youth that supported this alternative way of operating in the world.

Her parents married amid the civil rights movement in the country of the United States of America, in which racial tensions between black and white people were explosive. When her father, a white minister, started dating her mother, a black art teacher/artist, he was pressured to resign from the church where he was assistant minister. This marriage was a very unconventional union at a time when interracial marriages were still illegal in some areas of the country. Therefore, both parents held a soul desire to disrupt the systems and become trailblazers of unification consciousness, whether they knew it or not at a human level.

While her parents did not remain married, these qualities made them perfect primary influences for the embodied soul of Beki to activate her desire to become an agent of Awakening to the true nature of Oneness Consciousness, starting with herself. Her very physical existence as a biracial child went against what was "acceptable" during that time and activated the frequency of Oneness by disrupting this enforced division of the races.

Her stepmother, who married her father when she was nine, also embodied a consciousness that flew in the face of convention. She entered the Catholic convent to become a nun at eighteen, renouncing all worldly possessions and devoting herself to a life of serving the Divine. Later, after leaving the community, she questioned many aspects of the religious dogma that did not resonate with the essence of Love. She recognized the contradictions within a world that she also loved. This is a paradox that many, at this time on Earth, find themselves grappling with.

Each of Beki's parental figures embodied specific core frequencies that would encourage the development of their children to embrace their unique and authentic selves and follow their inner compass. Therefore, they received the message that it was a sign of strength and intelligence to question widely accepted paradigms and dogmas.

Beki made many choices throughout her life that did not conform to social norms and primed her to question the narratives of the chaos ensuing during the pandemic years. It was more challenging this time because the pressure to conform was ubiquitous. Before this event, Beki could follow her sense of knowing in a personal and undisputed way for the most part. The years 2020-2022 were challenging everyone in some way or another. Beki and others in the spiritual community she resonated with sensed that this was part of a collective contraction meant to accelerate the Awakening of humanity. While it was harrowing for many, with so much loss and hurt, it was divinely purposeful and necessary to shake up humanity in intense and diverse ways. Contractions are a potent tool for transformation. They can be gentle when there is little resistance. However, the more flailing, fearing and pushing against, the more powerful the contractions can be that inevitably bring forth the desired expansion and evolution of the self and the Whole.

NINETEEN

The Mystic Medium

Hōwaka-heh manya wali hee'ti
Hah'ku nanya tatata taa

Beki left the evening gathering that she was attending in the magical mountain retreat only four hours from her home by the sea. As she walked around the area, she felt a sweet resonance with the mountain air and the tall, lush trees donning flowers unfamiliar to the trees in the marshy lands of her home. She loved both. As she climbed the hill to return to her little room, she felt excited about this long-awaited appointment with a psychic medium that her friend had told her about months before.

Beki had always been drawn to teachers and information that came from non-physical entities. She felt they offered a clearer, less mired perspective on human follies. So, after twenty-plus years of exploring channeled material, it was surprising that she had never had a session with a medium specializing in talking with departed loved ones. At this point, Beki was accessing the Akashic Records for herself and with clients in her "Soul Sessions" and when creating Soul Portraits. While this work offered powerful insights and connections to the Divine Wisdom that included the energy of loved ones, she was eager to see how this experience would allow for another way to connect with her beloved father, who had made his physical transition in 2018, almost four years prior.

She sat with her computer screen, poised to receive the video call from Myrna. As she emerged on the screen, she greeted Beki with a lovely big smile, full red lips, a light brown complexion, flawless skin, and big brown eyes. She asked Beki what she could do for her. Beki simply let her know that there was someone she wanted to connect with. Immediately, Myrna said, tilting her head, "George Harvey?"

Beki was amazed! Her father's essence emerged and eagerly began to speak through Myrna. The first thing he expressed was to acknowledge Beki's non-conforming nature. He said that she always thought for herself, even as a young child, and that he always admired that about her. He shared details about his after-death experience and what he was learning in his new existence. The whole hour was filled with fruitful connections, laughter, and fascinating information about her father's experience of the other side.

Beki was so excited about this mystical exchange that she decided to schedule monthly sessions to explore this dimension of reality that Myrna seemed so easily attuned to. Each time they met there was a fascinating interaction that stretched her mind opening her to new possibilities. She particularly enjoyed her conversations with her father who seemed to be having quite an adventure. He told her that he specifically took classes in healing so that he could share with her what he was learning, knowing that she would find him and ask about it one day.

One time he shared with her that he had been on Safari! Beki leaned into the screen with curiosity. "Really?" she asked in disbelief. "Yes!" her father exclaimed. "It was extraordinary. You can walk right beside the animals because they are not afraid of us here. I can hear what they are thinking and know about their existence. It is not what you would think. It is life-changing. I promise you." He himself was clearly in awe of the experience. When Beki asked him if he would take her on Safari when she made it across the veil, his response surprised and delighted her. "Of course, but I am planning on taking you to the bottom of the Pacific Ocean. It is immense and it is filled with light. The same light where I live."

Then, one warm evening, Beki sat in her magical little studio preparing for her next session with Myrna, excited to see what would be revealed. She settled into her sacred space where she created art and initiated her Soul sessions combining the healing energies of Reiki, Akashic Records, and Flower Essences as catalysts for Awakening. The room was filled with her paintings and the floors were covered with beautiful red Turkish Kilims that she and her husband had purchased many years before when traveling in Turkey. While the space was small, it was rich with beauty, and the frequency of healing energies was palpable.

As Beki settled into her chair, ready to join Myrna on the screen, she felt a distinct sensation around her neck that felt like pressure. This was when Beki heard the subtle, inner voice letting her know there was someone new that she would encounter that day. As Beki shared this with Myrna she noticed a blue light surrounding her throat and head and felt the presence of someone strumming Beki's throat. Myrna quickly realized that this was a Soul Path Guide who called herself Namundhi.

This is the fateful moment in our story when Namundhi first became aware of Beki and her connection to Shahalaku as her soul-kin, seeing the opportunity to support her in her Awakening journey. At this point within eternity, Namundhi was not embodied. She was powerfully drawn to Beki because of this ancient soul connection in which they shared a beautiful life together as Numundhi and Shahalaku, fellow Priestesses and dear friends. Namunhi's passion was to support Awakening, not just during her life as the Hōwaka-heh but in All Time and Space. So, this was a perfect opportunity for her to activate Awakening in this beloved soul who also was seeking to be an agent of Awakening

This is the beginning of the journey with Beki when she is fifty-five years of age in her dimension of time. Once the initiation of Namundhi as Beki's Soul Path Guide began, Namunhi's OverSoul orchestrated the Memory of this moment to be transmitted to herself as a Priestess/Hōwaka-heh in her time with Shahalaku. Together they activated Beki's Awakening during many key moments throughout her entire life.

In this "first" meeting with Namundhi Beki received the initial activation of the Memory of her native language, Weeshah'aneylo. Myrna shared Namunhi's instructions on how to allow these *"word poems"* to form Soul Mantras for healing and transformation for those hearing and speaking the mantra. This would attune Beki to her lifetime as Shahalaku. The holy language would transfer the frequencies of Wholeness and Creation within the language of the Sacred Breath, offering a potent tool for herself and others for Awakening to Oneness.

For the following months, Namundhi continued to gradually attune Beki to this new and ancient frequency. This initiated the deeper levels of Awakening that she had been calling forth. Everything was coming together like a magnificent puzzle. It was an exhilarating adventure to merge these two realities, weaving in the vibrations of wisdom, knowing, compassion, creativity, *and* a powerful, untapped resource for Beki — imagination.

Both Namundhi and Shahalaku were excited to see how Beki would implement the transmissions being offered. It was ultimately her choice to accept this gift. It would require readiness, faith, confidence, curiosity, and courage to allow such a shift in consciousness to occur, allowing the evolution of her gifts to unfold in unexpected ways. She would have to conquer her nagging tendency to introduce self-doubt and her skeptical mind that had been trained to need tangible validation for everything to make it real, true, and acceptable.

Shahala and Namundhi knew that introducing this concept of the mantras too soon would simply be a wasted moment in which Beki would discount such an idea. Yet they had inserted enough symbols, signs, and experiences into her lifetime to create a receptivity around the ideas they would present. It truly was a work of art, this tapestry of love and infusion of Oneness that these Hōwaka-heh women created as they danced their magic into the life of Beki in collaboration with her Life Guides that had been supporting her from the very beginning of her incarnation.

Now, it was up to Beki to accept this gift and find a way to implement it in her world to support her passionate desire to aid in the Awakening of all!

CHAPTER 20

Soul Mantra

Iōwayah'ho lahlah mani'ti
Honata honata honata
Haa haa

Beki was excited to connect with this entity, who called herself "Namundhi." Myrna explained that she was her "Life Path Guide," which differs from the Life Guides, who are with you for your entire life. She continued, "This person takes a special interest in your path and has something to offer. Think of her like a vocational counselor."

Namundhi began her dialogue with Beki, *"The word poems which want to be birthed through you are a very particular and potent form of healing."* When Beki looked puzzled, she expounded, offering detailed instructions on this unique healing modality and how to bring this gift to her clients to support them by aligning them with their Soul Essence. Beki asked many questions, eager to understand how best to embody this wisdom. Through Myrna, Namundhi spoke of numerical values assigned to each word and how the healing frequencies within the words would initiate the energy of Wholeness.

Namundhi sensed Beki's confusion and determination to get it "right." She reassured her, *"This is not an exercise meant to challenge you unduly. It is meant for you to provide adequate answers to unwellness. The energy is understood by few. You have such an understanding."* Speaking through Myrna, she continued, *"I feel that the impact of a word poem is similar to hieroglyphics, or the characters found in Japa (a Sanskrit word). The word poem is a tool made especially for you."*

After Beki asked several more questions, Namundhi elucidated, *"This is a native language for you that you have spoken many times before. It is an aspect of future thought you have already encapsulated many times before. But the time in which you (now) exist has regressed."*

Beki, again, looked confused, tipping her head to the side. Myrna noticed this as she peered through the screen and exclaimed, "I get it! I get it! Namundhi means that even though she is speaking from an ancient "time," it is more evolved than our current time." Beki was beginning to follow the rhythm of Namundhi's words and ideas, although it felt somewhat foreign. Namundhi was new at communicating in the language of separation, common to the land and time of Beki and Myrna. Although they may not fully understand her, Namundhi knew that the frequency of the transmission she was offering would transcend her words and be received by Beki at a soul level.

Beki asked Myrna if Namundhi could speak the words of her language aloud. Myrna's skills in translating Namundhi's words fascinated Beki. As she listened, she felt a soft wave of electrified energy ripple through her body. She was immediately struck by how familiar the spoken words felt. She asked her to speak the word for "Soul."

Namundhi responded by pronouncing the word slowly and then repeating it. *"Iōwayah'ho. It is the Divine Breath out. It is the language of Wholeness and Creation, always with the Divine Breath out."*

Then she said something very profound, *"All illness is a dream you choose to participate in. Wholeness is when you choose to Awaken from the dream."*

Beki was intrigued. She shared with Myrna that she was already familiar with the word *Japa,* having heard it many years before when her mother had found out she had breast cancer. Beki's sister, Sarah, had taken their mother to meet with the guru of the Siddha Yoga Path during Darshan, with many hundreds of her devotees awaiting her presence. When her mother had the opportunity to share her condition with the guru and her dilemma of how to proceed, the guru simply said to her, "Do Japa!" Not knowing what that meant, Sarah quickly explained that Japa meant to *repeat the mantra*. The Siddha Yoga mantra is *Om namah shivaya*. Translated from Sanskrit, it means "Om, I bow to Shiva, the auspicious one, the supreme Self." It had also been explained to Beki as a mantra to honor the Divine Self within.

She remembered an interaction with Chrys, a Reiki master and Akashic Records consultant, many years earlier. Shortly after beginning a deep healing journey with Chrys, while in a session, Beki's Guides invited her to offer her clients a new form of healing. It would blend the potent energies of her art with her healing practices to create *Soul Portraits*. By accessing the Akashic Record of her client and calling forth their Soul, each painting would become a transmission of their Divine Self, which could be used as a tool for healing, evolution, and Awakening.

When Namundhi offered the idea to create these word poems as a potent form of healing to activate the essence of this ancient Soul Language of Wholeness and Creation, it reminded Beki of the Soul Portraits. At that moment, she decided to call these poems *Soul Mantras*. She immediately felt resonance with the idea as she already had a natural affinity for writing. It was a tool that she had used since she was very young to connect to the Divine. In her late twenties, she began to do "spirit writing," where she would receive channeled wisdom as she inquired for guidance. She would fill volumes of journals, not knowing what to do with them all but finding the practice highly beneficial to her understanding and evolution.

She mused at how Namundhi must have known this about her. Beki's skeptical mind occasionally whispered nagging thoughts of doubt, worrying about how others may perceive her strange meanderings into the wilderness of the unknown — the non-physical dimensions. Beki was accustomed to forging her own path and taking the road less traveled, so she did not allow her skeptical mind to hinder her enthusiasm to explore this new tool for healing and initiating Awakening.

Namundhi was pleased that Beki was so receptive to the suggestion. She wasted no time and immediately began experimenting with the Soul Mantras, writing them for herself, her mother, and her clients. She began to get positive feedback that let her know they were having an effect. They were simple, direct, and immediate. She was already finely attuned to the vibrations of words received from the Divine Realm and had been consulting the Akashic Records for herself and her clients for some time now. This gave her the confidence and trust that she could effortlessly receive the perfect mantra to offer as yet another creative way to align to the Soul.

Namundhi *and* Beki knew how critical this alignment was for the Awakening, of humanity. Alignment with the Soul allows one to see the Truth of their Beauty and Power and open to the awareness that they are the cause of their own life experiences, not the victim of them. If this could happen on a large scale, then the world literally could change overnight. People would stop empowering the beliefs that do not serve the creation of a reality and world of their desires.

Beki memorized her own Soul Mantra and chanted it throughout the day:

Stay
Feel Beauty enter your heart now
Tickle Love,
Be Love
Feel wisdom-infused cells now
All now,
here
Stay well.

It was simple, and Beki trusted it would do whatever it needed to shift the energies that did not serve Love and alignment with her True Self. Beki pondered the similarities of the mantras to the flower essences that she offered her clients to dissolve the static energies that specific thought patterns, beliefs, and emotions cause. The flowers flood one's auric field with *aligned* and *resonant* frequencies to achieve this transformation and healing to one's natural state of harmony and balance, returning them to their Soul essence. Beki had even developed the practice of writing an affirmation on the bottle of flower essences created specifically for each client, which resembled the emerging practice of creating Soul Mantras. The transition was seamless as she Awakened to this sacred frequency within her Soul Language.

Beki would intuitively write these short poems to be used as mantras and read them aloud to her clients. They would share their emotional or energetic response, letting her know when there was resonance. It was a wonderful exploration. Then, one day, at the beginning of November, Beki sent her mother a mantra that she channeled especially for her. Her mother told her that she loved the mantra and diligently attempted to remember it and repeat it as her daughter had instructed.

A strange thing happened one week later.

On November 7, 2022, Beki's mother, Elayna, called her on the phone, out of breath. Elayna was having chest pain that was similar to the sensation she had experienced when she had a heart attack over three years prior. Beki called an ambulance and drove to her house, just five minutes away. Her body shook with worry, but once she got there, she did her best to calm down enough to deal with the emergency. The ambulance took Elayna to the hospital, where she stayed a few more days as they monitored her and decided on a plan to treat her condition. The cardiologist decided to manage her condition with medication because he deemed it to be too risky this time to do an invasive procedure. While she still struggled with pain for a few days, eventually, she became more comfortable and began the journey of recovery. While the whole experience was traumatic, the family was grateful and relieved that she survived the episode.

Beki felt exhausted and very worried for her mother, who was such an integral part of her life. It was hard to see her weak and in pain. The two shared many interests, including the quest for spiritual and personal growth. They both were painters and loved to explore the world beyond form. Elayna was eighty-four then and had already outlived the mortality age of her parents and younger brother. Each day was precious. Beki knew she would have to let her go one day, but she also knew she would never truly be ready.

It gave her some sense of solace to know that she had found this wonderful medium to channel the soul of her father and others. She knew that she would have a direct line of communication through Myrna and that with the continued development of her own extrasensory perception, she could be in communion with her mom even after she left the physical plane.

Two days after her mother was hospitalized for the concerning heart symptoms, it was Beki's fifty-sixth birthday. Her husband offered to sleep at the hospital so she could go home and get some rest. Months ago, she had scheduled a meeting with Myrna for this special day, not knowing then how much she would need it at that moment. Needless to say, she was eager to receive some insight into what had just happened with her mother. She sat in front of the little screen, alone in her home, feeling worn out but also grateful that her mom was alive. This birthday could have been a very different kind of day.

Myrna's sunny smile emerged on her screen. It was a welcome sight. Beki commenced to tell her of the recent saga. She also shared with her that she had begun to offer the Soul Mantras to her clients and felt excited about the responses she was receiving as people started to work with them. Then she queried, with some confusion, why was it that after just one week of her mother receiving her mantra and practicing it in earnest, she would have a heart attack? After all, she thought the mantras were meant to be a source of healing.

Namundhi spoke through Myrna without missing a beat, *"You have given her room to stay. You have allowed her to stay longer in the human experience."*

Beki's mouth dropped open. "What? You mean…? Like, it was one of her potential departure points for her?"

"Yes, she felt the love for Self. She felt the love for family and the love for the experience through the words you painted on her soul."

Both Myrna and Beki were in awe. Wow, they marveled at the potential of these simple poems! With both disbelief and excitement, Beki shared with Myrna and Namundhi the Soul Mantra that she had given her mother:

> As I settle, sit, and **stay**
> in the space
> of Beauty
> that I have created
> I see beyond the veil
> to reveal the grace
> of that which cannot be seen
> yet felt in fullness.
> My eyes penetrate beyond the now
> and bring that Beauty to now.
> I am fulfilled.

They both looked at each other in recognition that something extraordinary had happened. It was hard for Beki to absorb. Myrna exclaimed, "Oh my God, your mother wasn't supposed to survive!"

"Is that really true?" Beki questioned again, feeling some of that old nagging doubt. "Could that be?"

Myrna spoke with excitement. "You healed her heart enough so it could withstand it (the heart attack)."

Namundhi also shared her wisdom by offering these words: *"It is not a case of the heart weakening. It is a case of the spirit beginning to strengthen. The spirit cannot be contained as easily as it used to be. There is no need to fear this process. Instead, take time to think about a spirit that is enlarging so quickly; what it is that this spirit needs to say to communicate; and what this spirit needs to experience. Ask those things, and you will come to a greater understanding of what has and will happen, and you will be at peace with both."*

Beki felt inspired and excited about the possibilities of this new healing modality and wondered how it would unfold. The rest of the evening, on her fifty-sixth birthday, she wrote Soul Mantras for her family members, who were all so concerned for her mother. She sent distant Reiki to her mother and her siblings along with text messages with the Soul Mantras infused with Love and trust that all was well.

TWENTY-ONE

Soul Language

Weeshah'aneylo
Wali maki hani'haa

Namundhi was pleased with how her transmissions with Beki were unfolding. She was thrilled with how Beki embraced the gifts of Memory that she and Shahala were infusing into her consciousness. She had told Beki that the language would Awaken within her in "time." Beki continued to communicate with Namundhi who had shared the actual words of the language with her so that it might help activate her memory. Myrna's ability to receive and translate the sounds Namundhi delivered to her was quite remarkable.

As Beki received the spoken words of Weeshah'aneylo, she felt a sweet resonance, indicated by waves of goosebumps cascading over her body. Namundhi marveled at the common mechanism of the bodies of the humans of this time and the beings of Hōlawai'kiki in the way their hair follicles would rise to receive the resonant frequencies like little antennae. It was a delicious sensation and an excellent indicator of alignment. This is a way that the non-physical world communicates and sends transmissions to loved ones and to those embodied souls that they serve as Spirit Guides.

As Namundhi consulted with Shahala about how they may best accelerate this transmission, they both agreed that it was time to introduce Shahalaku to Beki in a more tangible way. Shahala had not made direct contact since the Eagle Awakening, over a decade earlier in Beki's time frame. It had only been a few months since Namundhi made her appearance with Myrna. They had waited for the perfect opening for Beki to be ready to receive the next transmission. Now that Namundhi had introduced her Soul Language to her, Beki began to sense the essence of the self who inhabited the world that embodied the language of the Sacred Breath.

One day as Beki was walking in the park allowing these words, native to her soul, to dance around on her tongue, she heard the word '*Shahalaku*' clearly emerge in her mind. She whispered it aloud and knew instantaneously that she had spoken the name she called herself during the lifetime she shared with Namundhi. She was intrigued as she continued to chant her name along with other pleasant sounds that were feeling more and more at home in her body.

Not long after, Beki decided she would create a painting of Shahalaku. Beki used the inspiration Myrna had offered when she described how Namundhi first revealed herself to her during their session. A powerful and colorful image began to emerge on her canvas. The bronzy-golden locks shimmered on the canvas framing a gentle, yet piercing gaze. Her long neck was framed with feather-like shapes and an emerald jewel right at the suprasternal notch (the visible dip at the base of the throat). Yellow and green were the predominant colors of the adornments complimenting her reddish-bronze skin tone. She was pleased with the image and excited to share it with Myrna the next time they met.

While the language fascinated her and she could feel the urge to express it, Beki was shy about speaking it aloud in front of anyone. She could feel those sticky thoughts of self-doubt along with the protective voice of her ego warning her of danger. After all, what would people think? It was already enough to be who she was, with her non-conforming nature, but trying to explain this?! She did not even know exactly what was happening or what to do with it. Beki had limited exposure to the phenomenon known as Light Language and was intrigued by the sense of resonance she felt when first hearing someone speak it. Yet, it still seemed strange, and she sensed it would be best to keep this development to herself.

As Beki resisted and repressed, her body eventually started to let her know that she was not allowing something powerful to flow through her. By January, her ears were feeling strangely plugged or muffled. She was uncomfortably sensitive to certain sounds including the low tones of her husband's voice. Then one day, after many days of this strange sensation in her ears, she had an intense episode of vertigo. For two days she could not raise her head from her bed. She was miserable and could not imagine living like this. She sensed she was dealing with an energetic condition. She already had plenty of experience with this way of seeing physical symptoms. Yet, after several weeks of muffled ears, she decided to seek medical attention to make sure she was not dealing with some kind of literal blockage that should be addressed medically. Nope. Nothing. Perfectly clear.

Her healer, Chrys, told Beki that it was important for her to ground the higher etheric frequencies that she was consistently working within her healing work. She made some suggestions on how to do this and offered her Reiki. Within a few days, Beki noticed some definite improvement. However, after a while, the muffled sensation in her ears returned. When she finally met with Myrna again, Namundhi immediately made her presence known.

Namundhi and Shahala had been monitoring this activation of the Language of the Sacred Breath/Ha'mana observing the enthusiasm with which Beki embraced it while in private. They had hoped to avoid any physical discomfort that can come with a sudden shift of vibration. However, they did not anticipate her resistance to be as strong as her excitement. The clashing frequencies were causing a symptom that was making it uncomfortable for her to fully attune to the new frequency.

They decided they needed to offer another approach that would help support her in this process of attuning to the powerful energy of the Soul Language that carried a frequency of Light rare in this land of extreme polarities. Shahala decided to go into Ceremony to commune with her

OverSoul, the Soul Self that she and Beki share, to receive some insight on how best to align these frequencies with Beki's Life Plan.

TWENTY-TWO

Soul Communion

Wahanna Wah'halama
Ee'mani titi
Hōlima halima paca'watee

Shahalaku entered a beautiful sanctuary in one of her favorite places in the magical Land of Waterfalls. It would be the perfect place to offer a powerful container for initiating a solo ritual to commune with her Soul and receive insights on how best to serve this exciting new venture with Beki.

This sacred space consisting of an intimate, circular clearing was surrounded by a beautiful cathedral of tall trees. Indeed, it was a wonder to behold how these majestic trees reached toward the sky with branches arching in perfect symmetry creating a stunning canopy framing the space below. These branches were embraced by winding vines with the most extraordinary white blossoms resembling exquisitely ornate lanterns, donning a long, red stamen stretching out of the bloom's center with a bright yellow tip. If you touch the tip and bring the syrupy nectar to your tongue, it will taste like a mix of aromatic sweetness with a peppery aftertaste. It is a delicacy in the cuisine of Hōlawai'kiki that is used as an infusion for several of the traditional dishes, both savory and sweet. Its gift to the people is to allow their bodies to quickly assimilate nutrients into their cells while simultaneously flooding the mind with a sense of calm.

Some flowers are particularly stimulating to the body, and others enhance the faculty of imagination. The cuisine is as intentional in activating particular qualities of experience in the mind and body as it is in bringing nourishment and a sense of pleasure to the taste buds. There is a unique dance between the people and the plant kingdom. They are intertwined just as the vine wraps itself around the tree. The gifts the people offer the plants sometimes include consuming them and bringing the essences of gratitude, pleasure, and purpose to their existence. It allows a way for the plants to both serve and become transformed. Plant souls are much more aligned to the ethereal dimension; for many, their physical expression is more transitory, especially in the case of the blossoms. Yet many plants choose to outlive the bodies of most people so they can anchor the energy of timelessness to the land and witness the evolution and transition of life all around them. Of course, this is the case for many great and ancient souls embodying the trees.

This nature sanctuary always sent a shiver of delight through the body of Shahalaku. She was a great lover of Beauty, and no place felt more beautiful than this one. She took a deep breath as she entered the clearing covered with green clover, which beckoned her to sit and receive the sweet, soft embrace of the land. The air was drenched with the aroma of the blossoms enhanced by the morning dew. As Shahala began her ritual chant that called forth her Soul, she felt the energy and love from the flowers fill her lungs and usher her into the realm of Infinite Wisdom and Divine Love. While Hōlawai'kiki and this sacred spot were the home of her heart, she felt the intoxicating Home of her Eternal Soul beckon her. Her heart burst forth with an expansiveness that sent waves of goosebumps all over her skin, with each hair on her body reaching out toward the Beloved Self. In the space of no time, this endless embrace lasted forever.

Then, as the energy began to settle and Shahala felt ready to commune with her Soul by using the faculties of her mind, she asked her Divine Self how best to support her iōwayah'ho-kiki in the land and time of polarity, separation, and transformation. With no words, the Beloved Self penetrated her mind with the creative force of Love and Illumination, and immediately, Shahala knew exactly what she would offer.

Shahala stayed for a while, soaking in the frequencies of her Soul, absorbing the essence of the blooms and the plant beings that encircled her. She felt the playful nature of this land intermingled with a profound sense of reverence. When she stepped out to rejoin the others, her body was shimmering from the inside out. The infusion of her Light Self would have her glowing more brightly than usual for some time. Nourishment of Soul Communion is superior to anything one might ingest. The Hōlawai had created a world in which all pleasurable activities would be the way they would nourish their bodies and keep themselves strong, vibrant, and beautiful for as long as they choose to be embodied.

While immortality is an option for the Hōlawai, it is not what most choose to experience. Since they possess an extraordinarily developed imagination, they want to experience other worlds and dimensions that would require relinquishing the vessel meant for the world they inhabit and acquiring a new form. As much as they enjoy the Utopia of their creation, they recognize the benefits of new, unique, and diverse experiences that inspire the expansion of their creative abilities.

Since they do not doubt the continuation of life in new and extraordinary ways, they do not fear death. After all, they always choose the moment of departure from their body. So, this is not even seen as "death," as we know it. The word "transition" would more accurately describe their experience. It is a transition welcomed by the one choosing it, even though they may feel the emotions of sadness as they move away from their known world into the next dimension. Even this sadness is included as something precious to be felt and known. It gives dimension and sweetness to the experience of Being.

Choice is intrinsic to the Hōlawai, who value this as a necessary function of conscious creation. As they observe other worlds or tune into their Souls' Memories of their different incarnations, they can see how important choice is. When and where beings do not feel they have a choice, there is a greater sense of powerlessness and fear, which often leads to violence and atrocities unimaginable to the inhabitants of the Land of Waterfalls.

As Shahalaku observed, this certainly was true of Beki's world. It helped her appreciate the function of *conscious* choice and the knowing that her people retain. Yet, she is also able to appreciate how this world of polarity benefits many other beings by offering a platform for experience. This is achieved through observation or, for the more adventurous, through total immersion, by becoming embodied in a dimension of extreme limitation due to amnesia. She admired the bravery of those like her own iōwayah'ho-kiki. The more she observed the challenges faced by the people of Earth at this time, the more passionate she felt about empowering Beki to support others who desire to Awaken. This excited Shahala as much as it inspired Beki. The two were merging consciousness in a beautiful orchestration of Divine Will and Desire.

TWENTY-THREE

Shahalaku: The Loving Self

Ahh'ahoo'ah
lamaya'hah hasha
Shahalaku
Ēawayshee'ah

Beki shared with Myrna the painting she had created of the parallel self that Namundhi had told her about. She was excited to discuss the name she remembered as her own while she had explored this new, ancient language. She wanted to receive some confirmation that she was on the right track.

Upon hearing the lyrical name, Myrna said, "Wait, wait, Shahalaku, Shahalaku...I am hearing something..." Myrna raised her hand to wave as she acknowledged it was Namundhi saying hello. "She is saying you are reclaiming your language." Myrna translated her words with a cadence and intonation that would shift with each new person she would bring forth in the session. Beki appreciated the nuances she sensed with certain entities and the more obvious shift from one to another.

Myrna smiled and continued, "Namundhi is saying, '*This is the word you coined to describe the Loving Self, and you referred to yourself in the third person with this (word), and people would refer to you as this, as a title. It is a recognition of the Soul's true existence. And just as I said, the language is coming back to you.'"*

Myrna had an expression of awe on her face. "Wow! Are the words coming through?" she asked Beki, referring to the Soul Language.

Beki shared her excitement, encouraged by Myrna's curiosity and the information she was channeling. "Yes! As I walk in nature and sit in meditation, I let it come out of my mouth instead of keeping it locked in my mind. It feels strange and familiar at the same time. I am letting the sounds be a playful exploration. Yet, I feel quite shy about sharing it with anyone, although I had a client on my healing table recently and allowed it to emerge without holding back. It was quite powerful."

Myrna responded, "She (Namundhi) says she understands what you are talking about. She says that you were speaking a prayer (with the client) that you created and used before. The words are burned onto your soul."

Through Myrna, Namundhi spoke the beautiful frequencies of her soul's native tongue:

"Ahh'ahoo'ah
lamaya'hah hasha
Shahalaku
Ēawayshee'ah

Welcome back, oh favored one
Lover of the Self
Created in perfection
Dweller of Wisdom."

Myrna and Beki inhaled deeply the sweetness of this transmission of sacred words.

Namundhi continued, *"You speak well, but you are fearful of reclaiming. But if you speak directly, without fear of being watched, it comes quite fluidly."*

It was all very affirming for Beki and helped her settle some of the self-doubt and fear she was feeling about allowing the language to find a home in her current physical being. While she was still uncertain how to utilize this new frequency as a tool for others, she sensed how it could support her in her own Awakening. After all, this was allowing her to integrate more of her multidimensional nature. Indeed, this aspect of her Being holds a wisdom and knowing aligned with an Awakened state of consciousness she so deeply desired to ReMember now.

When she shared her symptoms afflicting her ears and head, including the bout of vertigo, Myrna immediately seemed to know what was happening. She told Beki that she was "attuning."

"It is like you are bringing in so many places, things, and experiences that you are clogging up. There is a huge amount of growth occurring. You are shifting rapidly, and your gifts are going to expand in big ways."

Myrna offered some practical suggestions on navigating these symptoms and shared that she had a similar experience as she was attuning years earlier. While she did not say precisely what Beki was attuning to, it made perfect sense to her. She knew she was becoming attuned to the new frequencies held within this ancient and familiar language — a language that carried a very different vibration from the world she inhabited now.

Beki sensed that she was in the process of integration and that the current vessel she embodied was attempting to align with these "foreign" frequencies. However, because of the resistance from her physical ego-mind, which felt afraid and protective, she was feeling discomfort in her body. Yet, Beki also felt supported by the guidance she was receiving from her Divine Guides, including Namundhi, and she was so grateful for Myrna and her gift of channeling this wisdom and love. She was committed to finding her way through this fascinating new terrain and was optimistic that she would heal and transcend her fears and self-doubt. It felt too important not to. For she knew that this was what she came to Earth for, and this path was paved by her Soul as a creative way to continue her journey of Awakening.

With determination and excitement, she continued.

TWENTY-FOUR

Releasing Resistance

Haa Ha'mana
Haa Ha'mana
Haa Ha'mana Haa

I breathe the Sacred Breath
that speaks the Love of the heart.

Each day, the words became louder in Beki's mind, and she would share more about what was coming through with her clients. The Soul Mantras (written in English) that she had begun to receive and offer to people several months ago were becoming more concise. They were often preceded by the sounds and utterances from the Soul Language she now knew as Weeshah'aneylo.

While the translations did not always make sense to her English-speaking mind, they made perfect sense to her quantum mind and Soul Memory that defied the logic of her current incarnation. While Beki was embracing this new healing modality, she still felt continued resistance to fully accepting it. She could not quite get over the worry of what others may think. Hence, the physical symptoms prevailed in spurts, making her feel spacey and ungrounded.

In another session with Chrys, Beki expressed her frustration with these lingering symptoms. Chrys translated a message from her Guides of the Akashic Records, who told Beki that if she did not allow the language to come through, it would find another way. Beki looked concerned with this suggestion.

"How so?" she inquired.

"Well," Chrys explained, "it could come through in less comfortable ways, such as involuntary body movements or verbally blurting it out without warning."

"Oh my!" Beki exclaimed. She was not at all comfortable with that possibility! She sincerely wanted to know how she could release her resistance.

Chrys responded, "You do not need to speak this language with everyone. It is a sacred Light Language offered for healing and Awakening. You can let your clients know that you have received the gift of Light Language and that you may be guided to share it at some point during the session. Let them know that it offers a healing frequency that holds a vibration of Wholeness and Creation."

This idea settled Beki. That felt easy enough to do. Chrys then offered Reiki to help soothe the symptoms and the resistance that caused them. Beki took a deep breath of gratitude for the many ways she felt supported.

Hala'wa
Hōli'wa
Mah'hanawa

I am Holy Whole.

TWENTY-FIVE

The Plan

Hai maki nani
Balawaka hani nani ki
Hōlimani halima
Hani nani ki

Namundhi and Shahala met under the Balawaka tree on the outskirts of the village. They feasted on its juicy fig-like fruit abundantly adorning the branches. They marveled at how their world is teeming with diverse delicacies available for all. They had observed how Beki would need to go to a large building to attain such nourishment that originally came from the Earth. They laughed at the absurdity of it all. It seems counterproductive to create a building to house the food that would need to be preserved with chemicals or cooling devices rather than have the food source available for all inhabitants to access directly from the land. Not to mention the need for the medium of money to exchange goods.

These were foreign concepts to the world of Hōlawai'kiki, where all needs and desires are met through the vibration of creation, which sources each person's hamanaku/gift of exchange to share freely with all those who seek their offerings. There is an organic and natural harmony within their way of giving and receiving that works so well they could not have imagined any other way until they witnessed it in this different dimension.

They could see how it became necessary in Beki's world for this medium of exchange called money to be used. Since so many resources have become too removed from society's hub, people cannot access simple and essential things such as clean water/iōwai and all forms of nourishment for the body. They also implemented laborious practices to build their dwellings that often included stacking families in boxes on top of each other in the most unnatural and unattractive way.

The Hōlawai civilization is based on both Beauty and function. Creation and Wholeness and the intrinsic knowing that they are One with the Creator and one with that which is created are foundational to their way of life. It is unthinkable for people to die of starvation or at the hands of another sentient being. So much of this world of separation was contrary to the wisdom they embody.

Without words, they shared these thoughts as they came together to contemplate the next step in their transmissions with Beki. Since their last meeting, Shahalaku had received insight from her Soul during the Ceremony in the magical grove of trees which she was eager to share with Namundhi.

Shahala could feel the power of the genius that flowed from the Divine Self and was overcome with love and appreciation for such communication and clarity, particularly since she had become so aware of the challenges that those in the time of Beki faced to stay connected to this Inner Wisdom. She could not imagine forgetting such a fundamental knowing about the very nature of their true existence.

Namundhi listened intently as Shahala shared the vision she received of Beki writing a book about the world of Hōlawai'kiki. Since it would not be her first time receiving a transmission in this way, Beki was already attuned to the process of writing a channeled book. Her first was a spiritual memoir called *Bare Beauty: My Journey of Awakening*. In truth, all inspired material is a form of channeling. The creative process and activation of imagination is how the Soul Memory is received. This can be transmitted in a very creative, inventive way using metaphor and

116

storytelling. It can also be expressed in practical and tangible formulas for more technical inventions. Or it could be more abstract, just as her paintings often were.

In Beki's case, the writing modality was a refined tool for aligning with the Divine and receiving clear transmissions of thoughts and insights. She had been using this tool of guidance for over twenty years, so she had become very comfortable with the process and trusted the information she received.

"Would this not be a perfect way for us to support her in ReMembering, Awakening, and attuning to the frequency of her True Self?!" Shahalaku knew that her own incarnation was the closest life Beki had ever come to living in harmony and Oneness with the Soul Self, offering an experience of the embodied self expressed as already "Awake." ReMembering the story and life of Shahalaku could thus become a powerful tool for Beki's Awakening. Her life was not simply a concept or distant possibility but a felt experience of Oneness — something that Beki had glimpsed many times throughout her life. The most profound Awakening she experienced was the time that Shahala infused herself into her body and mind the day the eagle flew into her world. Shahalaku felt that this new possibility of inspiring Beki to remember and connect with her iōwayah'ho-kiki, through writing a book, could offer a way to transform her and those around her. This ReMembering is what Beki had been asking for, intending, and focusing her spiritual practice on for much of her lifetime. How wonderful if she could immerse herself in the frequency of her own Soul's Memory connecting her to the world embodied by Shahalaku and Namundhi!

Shahala's enthusiasm was contagious. Namundhi could feel the fullness of this possibility and reveled in the beauty, synchronicity, and perfection of this unfolding plan. With Beki aligning more and more each day with the dimension they inhabited and with Shahalaku, through embracing her Light Language, she was surely ripe to receive this transmission.

The writing process and revealing of the Utopia that was a part of her own soul's birthright would soothe Beki's resistant ego-mind since it was accustomed to this creative way of operating within her consciousness. The soul of Beki would be intrigued and drawn to the activation of imagination initiated by the Hōwaka-heh. Beki had never considered herself imaginative, even as an artist, since she felt that her creativity was more of a function of allowing the Divine to flow *through* her rather than using her imagination to create.

Namundhi felt it was important to engage her mind in a way that allowed her to feel the magic and power of the faculty of imagination as they applied it in their Creation Ceremonies. This approach would merge the cultivated ability for Beki to receive Divine inspiration through words and painting with the untapped ability to engage imagination for a synergetic effect of aligning and Awakening Beki.

Namundhi and Shahalaku felt this would also be beneficial in soothing the symptoms that were causing discomfort, by giving the mind a way to focus the energy and engage Beki's sense of excitement and purpose. It truly was a brilliant plan. They prepared to send the transmission right away.

TWENTY–SIX

Imagination Awakened

Ha'mana Wah'halama
Hani waku
Takina takina Shahalaku

In Hōlawai'kiki, there are many ceremonies that the Hōwaka-heh preside over. It is an honor to perform the large ceremonies that unite the whole community for creation and celebrations. Creation Ceremonies are also performed in more intimate circles and sometimes with only one other. These one-on-one rituals are particularly potent for Shahala because she can feel the reflection of the other's soul more intensely within her being. This is as much a gift for her as it is for the one she serves, which assists with her own evolution while it simultaneously assists them with theirs. She loves how the hamanaku of each individual truly reflects the principle of Oneness — as you give, you receive; and as you receive, you give.

Similarly, the Sacred Breath/Ha'mana, the very essence of their language, is a gift of love and nourishment to the plant kingdom. When the grandmother tree receives this gift, she returns it with her own breath drenched with the frequency of oxygen, nourishing the beings that roam the land. This symbiotic exchange is a simple, elegant effect of living in harmony with your gift, fully embodied and shared. It is natural for the energy to flow in a circle.

Namundhi and Shahala prepared the ceremony to initiate Beki's hamanaku with the powerful faculty of imagination, which would enhance her ability to receive the inspiration to write a book to connect her more intimately with the world of Shahalaku. Just as in all the Creation Ceremonies, they began with the ritual of emptying Beki's mind, clearing and cleansing her mental field. Then they waited until Beki reached the delicate threshold that allowed her to feel the spacious dimension of the Ha'wahakakaya/ Infinite Realm.

Namundhi and Shahalaku prepared the room for the ceremony with exotic and fragrant flowers. They had spent all day foraging for the perfect blend of flowers that would activate and enhance the faculty of imagination. They filled a clear crystal vessel with iōwai/water and infused it with the blooms, creating a beautiful flower essence. Since Beki already utilizes flower essences in her healing practice, she was already attuned to this energy as a potent catalyst for transformation. Of course, the Hōwaka knew this as they tailored the ceremony to Beki.

They chose to begin the initiation at dawn when Beki would begin her morning ritual, which starts with drinking some pure water with a strong crystalline structure. It was the perfect time for the holy women to transmit the essence of the Sacred Falls into Beki's drinking water. This iōwai/water was used in all the Creation Ceremonies for clearing and cleansing the auric field, assisting in emptying the mind to allow for a potent communion with the Ha'wahakakaya.

Beki settled into a cross-legged posture to meditate for the next hour, giving the Hōwaka plenty of time to offer gentle waves of energy to deepen the connection with the Ha'wahakakaya. When they sensed Beki had entered a state of clear, empty bliss, they waited just long enough for her to anchor fully into that sensation. Then, in perfect timing, they transmitted the frequency of the sacred elixir of flower essences, blended to activate and enhance imagination, thus becoming the magnetic force to align her with her Soul Memory.

Beki's body began to buzz. Waves of goosebumps wrapped her skin with the most exquisite sensation. Beki was no stranger to such ecstasy during meditation, but this morning, it was particularly delicious. As she soaked up the sweetness of the energetic caress, she felt her mind open, and in an instant, she conceived a story about her parallel self, Shahalaku. She could sense the entire story without knowing the details of what would emerge. It was as though she became aware that she was pregnant with a new being that would grow and eventually emerge from the womb of Infinite Possibility.

With this stroke of insight, she shivered with delight. She knew she must write it down. She knew that it would become a book. She knew it was a gift that would activate her gifts. She knew it would serve as a way to offer her gifts to others in a manner that would soothe them into their Awakening. As she felt the knowing engulf her, she surrendered. Her ego's smaller, worried voice reminded her of the labor of writing a book – something she vowed she would never do again. With the loving support of the Hōwaka sending vibrational frequencies incomparable to anything known on Earth at that time, the tiny ego fears were simply not heeded. Beki could feel the expansion of her hamanaku, and it felt exhilarating. The transmissions of the story began to unfold quickly and effortlessly.

Within five days, Beki had completed the first seventeen chapters! As the story came to life, Beki felt an excitement fueled by the flame of her passion for self-expression, beauty, art, and the essence of Awakening to the True nature within ALL. Time and space opened up, with perfect synchrony, to allow her undisturbed focus to bring forth this creation.

Namundhi and Shahalaku simultaneously felt the exhilaration of this transmission of Love in the form of a book as they witnessed Beki's receptiveness to the activation. They continued to hold her in the illumination of her own Wah'halama/Soul Memory, which contains the template of the entire transmission for this book that you are now reading. They waited patiently with excitement to see what would come next.

TWENTY–SEVEN

Convergence

Bal'hi Bekee
Iōwayah'ho-kiki
Shahalaku shamani
Wah'halama Haa

Beki was amazed at how quickly the story of Shahalaku flowed onto the computer screen. With her memoir *Bare Beauty*, which she had begun seven years prior, she noticed an ease with the writing, as though she was transcribing something already written. Strangely, remembering her own life felt like dipping into several past lives even though she was only fifty years old when she began her spiritual memoir. She marveled at how difficult it was for her to remember so much of her life. When she wrote *Bare Beauty*, she had been instructed by her Divine Guidance to simply focus on writing the points in her life that activated an Awakening. It had become a way for her to remember and amplify these transformational moments. Also, it served to help her appreciate the many life contractions that became catalysts to these Awakenings, just as physical contractions during the birthing process bring forth a new life, literally.

With *Bare Beauty,* she had first received the impulse to write when she heard a voice in her head inform her that she was to write a book. It

123

was during one of her daily walks in the wooded park that she loved so much, not far from her home. Beki always sensed that when she stepped into that park, she was entering another dimension – a parallel reality distinctly different in frequency from the everyday world she inhabited. She could easily sustain her alignment with this more refined dimension while bathed in the energy of this beautiful world of plants.

However, this time, as she ReMembered the world of Hōlawai'kiki, she marveled at the synchronicity of it all. After twenty-eight years of operating her boutique, *Utopia*, she was now ReMembering a *"real"* Utopia, a memory felt as a transmission of Love and Beauty. What an extraordinary and brilliant orchestration. Her life felt like a puzzle with a million pieces coming together. She could finally see more and more of the whole, magnificent picture.

In her many years of working with her healer, Chrys, she had only recently begun to explore several of her "past" lifetimes. Most of these explorations were a part of the process of accessing the Akashic Records for guidance to bring awareness to the root cause of the resistance that seemed to block her from her desired expansion and evolution. All these incarnations revealed some kind of trauma to heal. In contrast, this life as Shahalaku offered a memory of a Utopian-like world of unparalleled beauty, harmony, Wholeness, and Creation. Why now? Beki mused. What was the shift that is now allowing this new and intriguing development?

Just as the question arose in her mind, Beki could feel the familiar knowing well up in her heart, and the voice of her Divine Guidance Awaken within her:

"Dear one, you know the answer. For you and we are One and the wisdom of knowing seeks expression through you."

Beki could feel the tingling waves of energy cascade over her shoulders as the sweetness of this voice engaged her contemplation.

"Each previous lifetime that we explored with you before now offered a powerful opportunity to look at how traumas, small and large, can become trapped in the cellular memory of your body, soul, and mind. It creates a network of experiences that make up the particular and distinct personality in each life. These parallel selves connect like an intricate web

of exquisite beauty. From the perspective of your OverSoul and the Infinite One, it is a masterpiece of Beauty and Love lived in fullness. However, it can be utterly devastating from the human or embodied perspective.

"We chose certain lives to reveal to you that were particularly activated during this life experience as Beki in ways that hindered your development rather than enhancing your wisdom. The process of exploring trauma in this way is purely for the purpose of integration so that the wisdom garnered as a result of this particular life drama could be used to enhance your evolution. Since we accelerated this process of clearing and integration of trauma over the past year or so, you were poised for a transformational shift into a new awareness."

Beki felt the resonance of this knowing that her Divine Guidance always inspired. It felt good to explore and activate this aspect of herself as Shahalaku, her soul-kin from another dimension. She was excited to be able to share a new way of being and living that she could bring back to the world of here and now.

Beki pondered her first meeting with Myrna the Mystic Medium less than one year ago when she had the most amazing communication with her father through Myrna's "faithful translation", as he put it. It was no coincidence that Beki just happened to be attending a retreat inspired and centered around the work of the author and modern philosopher Charles Eisenstein. His work was grounded in ideas on how to initiate within us and the community ways to create a more beautiful world. The book that initially brought him to Beki's attention was *A More Beautiful World Our Hearts Know is Possible*. This synchronicity did not escape her as she immersed her consciousness in the *Land of Waterfalls*.

Shahalaku, Namundhi, and their world were unfolding before her eyes as she remembered and inscribed their way of life, unknowingly weaving their paths with hers in ways yet to be discovered.

This is the point of convergence.

The iōwayah'ho-kiki sit together, in a timeless space, in the eternal here and now. Filled with eager anticipation yet grounded in deep peace, they await the creative ways Life will guide them to the next phase of this wild and wondrous journey of Awakening.

PART TWO ⊙

THE PORTAL

Aka Aka

Halanema Aku

Wee Shahala

Honi mali Kalima

Kaliwah Aku

TWENTY-EIGHT

The Two Become One

The two
the One
The Essence of the Self
expressed as two
sit in a space
seemingly wide and vast
between the other

And yet
with each breath
they breathe as one

With each inhalation
they taste the scent
of flesh embodied
in a now
beyond
and here

They are ReMembering
Becoming known
to each other
threading the Soul
ReMembering the One in All

The gentle breeze is cool, filled with the sweet scent of jasmine. Beki hears a whisper, feels a longing, senses a grief that is not her own...or is it? Waves of sadness seem to cause her heart to flutter. Or is it the fluttering that is ushering in the sadness? Her ears are full, heavy, and muffled, making her feel unsteady. The whisper brushes against her heart, which seems to struggle to find a rhythm. Again, she ponders whether this grief, a sweet and sultry sadness, is her own. She is unsure where it comes from. Her head feels heavy.

Through the ethereal realms, Beki invokes the presence of her Guide, Namundhi. Without words, she shares the emotional and physical discomfort she is sensing. As she feels the steady, gentle recognition from her friend's energetic embrace, her aching heart slowly finds a new rhythm. It takes some time to acclimate, and as it does, her breath steadies, becoming more balanced.

As Shahalaku felt this odd, unfamiliar sensation, she noticed it was akin to longing yet somehow it felt deeper and heavier. While longing for children has been the only thing close to this sensation for Shahala, she still felt a sense of possibility within it. She sat, quietly contemplating. This achy sensation made her feel like she was in a dark hole, a void of nothingness. Shahala wondered why this darkness felt so different from the black, sweet warmth of the womb of creation, which she often entered for

Creation Ceremonies. She considered that perhaps she was sensing emotions that belonged to her soul-kin inhabiting a different perception of consciousness. They have become more aligned with each other's frequencies as of late. With fascination, she noticed her heartbeat becoming irregular. It was seeking a balance, and when the tears began to roll from her eyes unexpectedly, she felt a synchronization of the heartbeat.

Her beat began to dance in step with Beki's heartbeat. She felt the distinct moment it happened and took a deep breath to help establish a consistent rhythm. It reminded her of when she entered Beki's embodied soul when the majestic eagle came to her many years ago in Beki's time. Yet, in that case, she was the one shifting the frequency within Beki. This time, it was a meeting, a recognition of each other. They were both aware of the other. They both had something to offer the other.

Beki did not expect this. She felt that she was the only one to gain from this ReMembering. She thought it was Shahala, along with Namundhi, aiding *her* in this Awakening journey. What could she possibly have to give? After all, it was she who was lost in the world of separation and Shahala who lived in the world of embodied Oneness. Shahala, too, was surprised by this development.

They both sat
breathing the Sacred Breath
together
as One

"Oneness is now finding a home in the merging of the selves. The worlds are coming together, and a greater truth seeks to be felt."

"What is that greater truth?" they both ponder as they feel these words enter their minds.

The whisper tickles the insides of their ears, *"Truth cannot be known until it is experienced. Continue to follow the path that unfolds before you. Stay Awake, and you will know, feel, and ReMember beyond the now that each of you inhabits."*

Twenty-Nine

Ecstasy

Ha'mana haa
Ha'mana haa
Hōlamakini
Ha'mana ha ha

Shahalaku wandered through the lush verdant gardens just outside her village on the side of a hill. The raking light of the rising sun cast a glow upon her bronze skin and illuminated her wild locks. She had a dazed look in her green and yellow cat-like eyes. She was feeling the emergence of something new in her, and she couldn't quite figure out what was going on. She was contemplating the cryptic whisper that had offered a message to her and her iōwayah'ho-kiki, wondering how this realization would unfold.

Something begins to stir inside her as she feels the sensuousness of the air. Her heart feels warm in a way that meets the warmth of the sun as it slowly heats the cool air. She feels more aware of her body — how her hips move, and her long, slender legs feel as they climb the hill. She touches her skin, admiring how soft it is as her loins begin to quiver. She breathes deeply, stretching her neck, tipping her head back to allow the sun to caress her face, sensing her thick, long, soft locks brushing against her bare back.

Her heart skips a beat as she senses an erotic fire build at the base of her spine, warming the sacred space within her where life emerges. Her chest heaves to open to this wild heat as she feels the curve of her full breasts dance with the movements of her body. Each time her bare foot meets the ground, she is delighted by the energetic pulsation that she feels originating from the Earth, entering the soles of her feet and moving through her body like a wave of love. The tingling in her yoni gives rise to a throbbing.

Shahala is amazed by this sensation. It is like nothing she has experienced in her life. She wonders if this is what others feel when they come together in sexual union with another being. How could it be that she is suddenly feeling this without any initiation by another? She was mesmerized by the intensity of this erotic energy and the way it was becoming more and more centered within her genitals.

She was familiar with the ecstasy activated by her Soul Ceremonies, which enveloped the body with energetic waves that penetrated each cell with a feeling of union and merging with the Divine. However, it was unusual, in her world, for the Hōwaka to take a sexual partner. It was not a rule, as it has been for many other traditions and cultures across many time frames and dimensions. It was simply an unspoken understanding. It seemed that the Priest/esses were so perfectly satisfied and nourished by the communion with the Divine that it mitigated the more common desire for sexual union with another. The Eros of Divine Love was so powerful that the urge to engage in erotic love with another being was simply not as compelling.

What caught Shahala off guard was how she became consumed by a wild longing to connect with another being to fulfill this erotic fire. She innately sensed that if she were to join with another, the fire would find its fullness and be quenched. This primal energy aroused her physical body in such an extraordinary way. She was fascinated and very curious. For the first time, she yearned to be held in the arms of another, penetrated by the warm flesh of a lover.

As she surrendered to this intense ache, she felt an ecstatic trembling of her whole body as an orgasmic release took her to her knees. Waves of energy rippled through her, radiating from her vulva. It was sublime, completely encompassing, and utterly disconcerting to her, all at the same time. She had never felt as aware of every inch of her body as she was at that moment. She rolled onto the warm, wet, grassy ground and felt the embrace of the Earth hold her as she quivered with this sweet, new sensation.

She began to laugh aloud, and just as she did, a flock of pink birds took flight from a massive Babaya tree not far from where she lay. Her laughter became louder and echoed throughout the land.

THIRTY

Sexual Union

Hōlamakini
Mee wah palwaha
Eekiki nani mali malawa'ha

Beki sat with her laptop in front of her, pondering the story unfolding on her screen over the last few months. She contemplated the life of Shahalaku. So much had been revealed about her work as a Priestess. Of course, the Hōlawai did not even have a word for *work*. She loved the idea that each community member offered their unique gift or hamanaku to the Whole and how this was valued as an exchange of love. While Beki loved to learn the details of Shahalaku's hamanaku, she also had been wondering if she had a lover and if that was acceptable within her culture to be both Hōwaka *and* in a romantic relationship.

Beki cherished her relationship with her beloved. It offered deep connection and intimacy, unique from any other kind of relationship. She loved the organic and natural expression of love through sexual union and could not imagine a life without this kind of connection. She also appreciated the sharing of life responsibilities, not the least of which was the intense role of parenting. While they did not always agree on what was the best approach to parenting, her husband's commitment and love for their sons were undeniable, and their personal styles complemented each other exquisitely. Witnessing him as a father filled her with gratitude and immeasurable respect.

After forty years of knowing each other, they had found a wonderful, harmonious balance in their union. Her love for him continued to grow deeper with time. It was truly a reflection of the self-love she had cultivated within herself. The decades of inner spiritual and personal development allowed her to experience her beloved from the eyes of Self-love. While she knew she would never fully understand his innermost, intimate musings, she could always sense the essence of his Being. In her understanding of *Oneness*, her union with him was equal to her union with herSelf. The more she embraced her Divine Self, the more clearly, she could see and feel the Self that was him, and at the same time, one with her.

She was grateful that the sexual chemistry between the two of them never waned as they aged. They maintained a core attraction sustaining the ups and downs of life with all its mundane and unromantic necessities. Beki wondered what that invisible force of attraction was all about. Was it simply a primal function for the survival of the species, supported by chemical hormones and pheromones to ensure the attraction needed to procreate?

Beki contemplated a more romantic and fanciful notion that resonated with her more. She imagined that she and her husband had spent many lifetimes together exploring different forms of relationships: friends, siblings, colleagues, parent and child, etc. In some lives, they were ascetics or holy beings who chose to be celibate. Then, when they decided to come together in this life, they chose to be lovers. They intended it to be a lasting relationship since they both had experienced lifetimes with less stability and consistency. To be confident they would sustain this partnership, they ensured that a special ingredient in their bodies and souls would make them eternally attracted to each other.

Beki smiled at the way her imagination would wander and ponder. She liked to explore the meaning of life and felt she could find a richer explanation for everything. Recently, she heard a metaphysical teacher say that life was meaningless and that giving meaning to all life circumstances was up to us. A friend once told her, "What you believe, you make real to feel." Since she resonated with this perspective, she felt it best to *decide* what definition she would give to her life circumstances rather than letting someone else do it. She had come to embrace the idea that her thoughts, beliefs, feelings, and actions were the fodder that created her reality. When something was showing up in her reality that was not in alignment with her desires, Beki chose to practice self-inquiry to consider what unconscious beliefs or thoughts may be influencing the unwanted reflection. This required constant vigilance. It was so easy to get swept away in the drama, chaos, and negative expressions in her world and to slip into the cycle of victim-villain-savior.

In her past, she had subconsciously taken on the altruistic role of the savior. She learned this skill at a young age to navigate the emotional "mind-field" of her childhood. She unconsciously felt that she would be safe if she could ensure that everyone around her was emotionally well, happy, and peaceful. Most humans of her time and space will acquire some skill to cope with their world of polarity and separation. However, what works at one point can become a hindrance later in life.

Beki had worked to become aware of the unconscious patterns and beliefs, which caused dissonance, dis-ease, and all forms of discomfort in herself and others. This is why she was naturally drawn to the specific vocation in which she supported others to become free of these limiting thought patterns. Once the light of awareness reveals the false self, the emergence of the True Self becomes more and more effortless.

As Beki closed her computer, she contemplated what would be next in her story about Shahalaku and the enchanting Land of Waterfalls. She wanted to be faithful to the Soul Memory activated by the imagination inspiring the unfolding of this story.

With that thought, she felt her body quiver. She drew in a long, slow, deep breath.

"Shahala, is that you?" Beki asked aloud when she felt a whisper in her mind.

Goosebumps cascaded over her shoulders, and a tingling sensation roused within her erogenous zone. Beki smiled in recognition. The presence of her soul-kin was palpable. Shahala's erotic longing penetrated time and space. At that moment, Beki sensed that Shahala had an Awakening of her own to experience that Beki, despite the density of the world she inhabited, would help to initiate.

Simultaneously, Beki realized that Shahala had come not only to serve and give but also to receive the gift that Beki had to offer through her own presence and life experiences. Beki now understood what the Hōlawai have known forever: All Life is an eternal circle of giving and receiving. In Oneness, there is no *other*. All are One, and the One is All. Beki felt a sense of appreciation for this visceral realization. She was honored that her presence could support Shahalaku in *her* evolution, just as she has been an invaluable gift to her own Awakening.

Haa Whya Whoo
Hali mani walah haaa
Haa Whya Whoo

Deep Breath

THIRTY-ONE

Blending Hamanaku with Eros

Ha'mana Shahala
Ha'mana haa
Hōlamakini Shahala haa

Shahalaku sat up in the clearing of the green mountainside. Her view allowed her to behold the magnificence of three of the great waterfalls in Hōlawai'kiki that she so loved. She began chanting a sultry song that danced out on the breeze, meeting the wildlife surrounding her with a kiss. Each word emanating from the Sacred Breath offered nourishing elements to feed the trees and plants of her land. The Hōlawai are always aware of this symbiotic exchange as they embody an organic sense of intention and knowing with each voiced expression.

She pondered this powerful, yet sweet, interchange of energy that so many take for granted in the world of her iōwayah'ho-kiki. She imagined that the beings that partake in the hōlamakini (sacred act of sexual union) must feel a similar sense of reverence and pleasure for this intimate sharing of life force. Her body was still feeling the tingling sensations from this unexpected visitor of her ignited erotic flame. As she contemplated what had happened, she had a sudden realization.

Now that Beki was aware of Shahala, they were both experiencing the influences of their unique essences. Shahala had witnessed Beki's life, including the beauty and challenges of family life, something that she had not yet experienced in her own lifetime. While she had felt the yearning to be a birthing mother, she had not acknowledged a desire to explore sexual union with a lover. As already mentioned, it is not common for the Hōwaka to engage in hōlamakini, for it was believed that it would require too much energy and take away from the powerful container needed to act as Hōwaka for the whole community.

Why now would she be given this activation of the erotic fire? Shahala decided to go to her mentor and friend, who has been integral to her interaction with her iōwayah'ho-kiki. Perhaps she could offer her some understanding and guidance on what was occurring.

Namundhi's broad smile, baring her signature large white teeth, sparkled as Shahala walked through the threshold of her abode. Namundhi lived on a glorious expanse of land on the side of the mountain with breathtaking views of the range of mountains surrounding the valley. She had created a very simple, yet regal dwelling built into the sloping rock that slightly protruded from the mountainside. It was incredibly artistic and rivaled the most esteemed works of architecture in all time and space. Since the Hōwaka were only limited by their own imagination to bring forth their creations, there were many extraordinary homes in Hōlawai'kiki. The organic technologies born of the consciousness of the Hōlawai were much more efficient than the cumbersome technology of our time. It was elegant, simple, and instantaneous to create, and always in harmony with the Whole.

Shahala blushed with a sly grin as she walked into Namundhi's home. She paused, inhaling the spicy, sweet scent of simmering soup on the stove. She loved Namundhi's cooking. This artistic activity brought much joy to those who partook in her nourishing delicacies. She also taught others the art of preparing plant medicines passed down from their ancestors. It was an integral part of her hamanaku and one of her unique expressions as Hōwaka-heh.

Of course, her mentor already knew what Shahalaku was coming to discuss. It is common for the Hōlawai to use telepathy to communicate. Yet, because their spoken language is considered a sacred act of Love, which emanates the frequencies of Creation and Wholeness, the people continue to use it and keep it alive.

Namundhi was sensing this development even before Shahala was aware of it. She understood that as they intended to activate the frequencies of Oneness into the world of Beki for her Awakening, the part of Shahala that had not yet fully integrated and allowed Wholeness and Oneness to be embodied would be revealed and activated. After all, Beki and Shahala are a part of the same Soul. Once full awareness of each other was anchored, the powerful process of evolution from their distinct perspectives would bring Awakening to them both.

Namundhi knew this would happen but did not know exactly *how* it would unfold. She was delighted to see Shahala's radiant energy when she entered her room. She asked her to share her feelings as they considered the possibilities and potential for a greater level of growth and expansion due to this new sexual Awakening within Shahalaku.

With excitement, Shahala recounted the exquisite sensations of the erotic fire consuming her, bringing a new kind of ecstasy to her physical body. Even speaking about it reignited the memory in her body. She was eager to explore this erotic energy and was intrigued with the thought of taking a lover and perhaps surrendering to a new kind of love.

Namundhi explained to her that her iōwayah'ho-kiki had offered the activation of this possibility within Shahala because Beki herself was living a life that included romantic, sexual love. She explained to her that this sexual energy was a powerful force that could ignite the creative flame when the heart center was open. In the time of Beki, the activation of Eros aligned to Love was one of the most potent activations for Spiritual Alignment. Yet, because of the intensification of polarity consciousness, it can be an equally destructive force when it is disconnected from the heart center. It can be used to inflict great pain and desecrate the very seed of creation that it is meant to ignite.

Namundhi continued with excitement:

"Don't you see, my sweet sister, when you bring your own unique experience to the hōlamakini from this dimension, where we live with open hearts and sacred breath, how it will offer a new, unique quality to the erotic frequency, not only within you but into Beki's world through her? She is already aligned with this awareness and is deeply committed to her beloved. The combined activation of each of your unique perspectives can offer expansion in both realities.

"It is time for us to acknowledge that the tradition of the Hōwaka-heh to abstain from hōlamakini is perhaps outdated. I feel it is time for us to consider exploring how we, Hōwaka, can experience the erotic fire and bring the creative frequency, unique to it, to our hamanaku. Just as I have incorporated my love of cuisine integrating it into the plant medicines of the Hōwaka, how might you explore this gift of hōlamakini and integrate it into your gifts? Consider how this will enhance your understanding of the beings you tend to: the birthing mothers/wa'kamema and the wala'koko/fathers. Imagine what new energy could be incorporated into our creation rituals within the whole community.

"Hōlamakini is a very embodied frequency. It is full of the fire of manifestation. If you embrace this possibility of opening to your Eros in a way that includes a partner to explore the depths of this energy, you will be able to inspire more of our young ones to embrace the path of Hōwaka."

Shahalaku was inspired by Namundhi's excitement and how she framed this activation as a dynamic opportunity for the evolution of her people. Namundhi also expressed that integrating all aspects of the Self was a way to mirror the Oneness that Beki longed to understand. Shahala had not realized that she, too, had much to learn about embodying the consciousness of Oneness. She had taken for granted her relationship with the Memory of Oneness. Indeed, as she observed the dimension of Beki's time of extreme polarity, her world was a glowing example of Oneness. Now, it seemed ironic that Beki was becoming a catalyst for her to recognize a way in which she also could evolve into a greater expression of Oneness by integrating her sexual nature with her role as Hōwaka.

She was open and excited to receive any other insights that might come through this interaction from this other part of herSelf. For now, she had much to explore and learn about this erotic flame that was newly ignited in her. She marveled at the way life never ceased to amaze and delight.

THIRTY-TWO ☉

Haka and the Crystal Dome

Chaykhana Takai
Sahee wa'kamema
Hakamani balee wa'hai

In this beautiful land of falling water and lush green mountains, with beings who ReMember, embody, and speak the Sacred Breath of Oneness, Wholeness, and Creation, the coming together of lovers is a conscious act of creation. It is a unique art form to call forth a mate that will offer the qualities desired in a mutual and organic way. Both beings must align with the essence of this collaboration of energy and Love.

There are many ways to practice the art of Creation for the attraction of this entity to come to fruition. Some do a solo Hōlimama-Fafui/Creation Ceremony if they are adept at this practice. Others go to the village "matchmaker" or Hakamani, who specializes in this area of co-creation. She is kin to the Hōwaka-heh but more specialized in her hamanaku. Shahalaku always admired the accuracy of her matchmaking. Although she knew that she herself could perform the solo Creation Ritual to initiate this union and explore the world of erotic Love, she was curious and excited to receive the assistance of this skilled being.

Shahala entered the dark, dome-shaped room illuminated by glowing, smooth, polished crystal walls, alive with their own souls' energies. The dwelling of the Hakamani was carved into the base of a mountain filled with quarries of crystalline rock. The crystals emanated unique frequencies of color and light, casting a soft and sensual hue within the space.

Shahala immediately sensed the caress of Love and Beauty from these inanimate crystal entities radiating and filling her body with their essence. The aroma of sandalwood and patchouli with a hint of cinnamon floated through the room. Shahala observed a wall of scented oils labeled with the names of many local plants. Another shelf held a large selection of blended potions made from various matter, including the nectars of plants and animals. Luxurious, velvety cushions were placed on the ground surrounding a circular, exquisitely hand-carved table. In the center of the table was a transparent crystal sphere.

Offering a warm drink of cinnamon-infused cocoa, Haka (as the villagers fondly called her) gestured that Shahalaku take a seat. She sipped the drink, feeling the warm, thick sweetness flowing through her body. She sensed the circulating pulsations of her blood as the heat from the liquid left her throat and entered her chest. A gentle, tantalizing sensation arose in her womb and yoni. This delicious, sensuous fluid had reignited her sacred flame.

Haka smiled as she observed the Awakening of passion in this beautiful, young Hōwaka-heh. She not only offered the service of helping people to create and attract the appropriate partner, but she was a master in the art of Sacred Sexuality. Many would come to her for guidance in activating and enhancing their skills in deepening the erotic connection, expanding the Love that radiated from the sexual center as well as the heart center. Both types of Love incorporate the other, yet they radiate from different centers and origins. It is natural for most people to recognize the emotional love that arises from the heart center. So, for some, they must learn to recognize and channel the love energy through the sexual center and then allow it to flood the whole being with its signature frequency. This offers the most significant activation of sexual pleasure and a deep connection to the beloved.

While sexual union/hōlamakini is natural and innate for couples in love, deepening this exchange and inner experience through the art of sacred ritual offers the potential for greater expansion. Many in the community utilize this innate quality within their bodies and beings as a tool to activate expansive communion with the Divine. This art form can be practiced with a partner or alone. When done in a sacred container of intention and Love, it can be very potent to activate this inner erotic flame in a group as well.

While Shahala was aware of several of the practices within this domain of sexual union and expression, she was a complete novice and felt just a bit shy about how to proceed. All she knew was that she had a wild longing to feel this ravishing energy being met by another. So much of her communion with the Divine had been an intimate solo experience. She had always felt very content in being alone. Her social life mainly consisted of offerings she led in the community and on a one-on-one level of sharing. She was not attracted to gatherings that were void of purpose. She found herself easily bored and, at times, awkward with the mundane activities of life. For Shahalaku, the sacred and holy within All fed her most. It was natural for her to dance with the Divine while alone in nature or during holy ceremonies. This is why her chosen hamanaku perfectly matched her True Essence.

She remembered the story Namundhi would share about her when Shahala was very young. She loved to go where people were cutting cinnamon dancing with its dust, thinking it was dancing with her. Namundhi mused at how Shahala would visit others and unknowingly shake off bits of healing cinnamon in their presence, which revitalizes the life force and adds sweetness for those grieving. With fondness and recognition, Namundhi would say, *"Yet another aspect of your dancing, yet another aspect of your healing, working together."*

Her mentor shared with Shahala how she immediately recognized the innate healing qualities within her as a child and knew that she would one day be her teacher. As she observed this whimsical being who would speak to water and dance with cinnamon dust, Namundhi would marvel how she could guide her to harness her innate energies in a way that would bring

149

great Beauty and Love to the community. Namundhi frequently expressed her appreciation and joy in mentoring the young Hōwaka-heh.

Now, Shahala sensed the trajectory of her path had come to a fork in the road, for there are infinite realities that we can choose to align with. The expected course for the Hōwaka-heh had been to remain celibate and childless, serving the community in matters of the sublime and divine, creating and restoring Wholeness, and aiding in life transitions. The hamanaku of the Hōwaka was a beautiful and consuming vocation that Shahala loved. Yet, this Awakening of the erotic flame felt so powerful and intriguing that she knew it must be allowed and followed.

She was also grateful that her beloved friend and mentor, Namundhi, had counseled her to follow this path. Not just because it was natural and exciting but because it would offer an expanded experience and embodiment of Oneness both personally and collectively by trailblazing a new way for the Hōwaka.

In this crystal dome of exquisite beauty, Shahala pondered these things. At the same time, she marveled at the deliciousness of this sexual energy that was igniting a completely new appreciation for her body. She giggled when she sensed the mischievous gaze of Haka, who, like all the Hōwaka, could easily read her mind. Haka, too, could sense the possibilities within the shift in the old paradigm that limited the ability of the Hōwaka-heh to experience a deepening richness of embodied life. She was eager to assist with this evolution, not just for Shahalaku but for the Whole. For indeed, All are One, and One is All.

One is All
All are One
When I embrace
the heart of
the other
I am
Whole

Hala'wa
Hōli'wa
Mah'hanawa

I am Holy Whole.

THIRTY-THREE

Expanding to Include

Piasta kokoma Hōlima
Hene kakina
Takawa ha

Beki sat at the little blue mosaic table on her back porch overlooking the glorious garden that her husband, Sherman, had created and tended with great love. Planting and caring for the plants, both edible and decorative, helped him to drain away his worries and responsibilities during that precious time of connecting with nature's creation. Beki loved the paradise her beloved created in their suburban neighborhood on a barrier island close to Charleston, South Carolina, not far from the Atlantic Ocean. Just as he was the visionary of their outdoor sanctuary, she had created an inner home of beauty filled with her colorful paintings and soft, comfortable furnishings rich with sensual textures and tones. When one entered their unassuming 1960s ranch-style brick home, they'd often be surprised by the bold, artistic expression, which was far from ordinary. The walls were painted in rich, bold colors: deep crimson red, calming aquamarine, lavender, teal, and turquoise. They perfectly enhanced Beki's vibrant, sensual paintings that filled the home with a powerful vibration to activate the Soul and arouse the body.

The synergy between Beki and Sherman was evident in how they created a space of beauty inside and out, as well as the unique way they brought a balance of energies into their interactions with each other and with their sons. While Sherman tended to much of the more grounded and practical needs of the family, Beki was the one to bring the esoteric and spiritual qualities of exploration into the family dynamics. He offered her a deep sense of belonging and grounding that assisted her with navigating some of the density of Earthly life. She infused the soulful vibrations into the space with her art, her love of Beauty, and her desire to dive deep into the unseen realm of Divine Love embodied.

As parents, they each offered these distinct qualities to support their sons as they developed into young men. Now, they all live outside the home, with the youngest still in college. As their sons were forging their paths, Beki and Sherman were discovering a new way of being parents to young adults as they evolved in their own journey with each other, as a couple and as individuals. It was a rich exploration. Beki enjoyed getting to know her sons as they grew more and more into themselves. She was always fascinated with their unique expressions of being. With great interest, she observed the nuances of their emotional and physical well-being, while Sherman focused on the pragmatic concerns of life, carrying the responsibilities that Beki found laborious.

Beki had understood the catalytic power of her path as a mother and wife. These relationships were an intricate part of activating her soul's journey as a healer, which came to fruition as she entered her forties. The mother-role was particularly potent in revealing the unconscious limiting patterns that hindered her from truly experiencing Unconditional Love and Unconditional Peace.

A mother's love is often perceived as unconditional. Yet, ironically, Beki observed that it was with those that she was most attached that she tended to be most conditional. Because of her intense need for her sons to be happy, healthy, and free, if they were not, she would become consumed with worry and fear, which is not actually love at all. She had come to realize that when she could maintain her alignment with Divine Love regardless of the conditions of their state of being, *all* parties involved would benefit from the power of this Unconditional Love.

She was only entirely free of this more ordinary, human, conditional way of loving when she had the Eagle Awakening. This exhilarating state of being and her profound sense of presence and intimacy revealed a sweet awareness of what it was like to love another, unattached to the conditions surrounding them. It was sublime and deeply empowering to transcend her critical mind and experience the exquisite Love of the Divine Heart.

While Beki recognized that as she navigated these primary relationships with all the challenges and sweetness they contained, there had been a strange nagging belief that would occasionally surface. She wondered if it was truly possible to fully step into her soul's purpose and Divine self-expression while being married and tending to the needs of a family. This belief did not make rational sense to her even though she could see where it may have originated within the collective history of people who devoted their lives to the Divine, such as Priest/esses, monks or nuns, gurus, spiritual teachers, and the like. The tradition of sacrificing the more human, carnal expression of sexuality and the demands of having a family to devote oneself to spiritual life were sprinkled throughout history and modern times. She would sometimes wonder where that nagging came from. Perhaps a past lifetime? Mostly, she would push the thought away because it did not resonate with the life she was choosing to live.

Another insecure thought that was primarily dormant recently surfaced with the emergence of her Soul Language and the oddness of speaking these multidimensional words that she did not even fully understand: Would her husband finally think she had lost her mind? Already, they were so different. She sometimes feared that if she revealed some of the more peculiar aspects of her esoteric path that reflected her True Essence, somehow it may cause a distancing in their communion. At the same time, she knew her ego was trying to protect her from loss and being an outsider. After thirty-seven years of marriage, her husband had only demonstrated his unwavering acceptance of her and all her eccentricities.

When she experienced the Eagle Awakening so many years before, she had the powerful insight that it was her own conditional way of loving that she had projected onto her husband. From this Awakened state, the Unconditional Love she experienced with him was as transformative as it was with her eldest son, who at that time was the one to trigger her fears and worries most often. She remembered how liberating and exhilarating it was for her to unapologetically express to Sherman her desires and thoughts about their son without needing him to agree, validate, or feel the same way. Simultaneously, she felt an extraordinary sense of appreciation for his distinct way of dealing with their son. This was something that had been causing a great deal of tension between them. The liberation she felt affected absolutely everything. At that moment, she needed nothing from anyone to feel Whole.

In her subsequent contemplations, she recognized that her fear that she and her husband could not be together if she was fully transparent about her unconventional ways of thinking was not even about him. It was her projection and fear of what it would mean to step off the cliff and trust in this wide and wild field of the unknown. The known world of form was visible, tangible, and accepted as "real" through collective consensus. She secretly feared whether she would still belong, be accepted, or acceptable, in the world of her reality, if she allowed herself to explore what kept showing up in her consciousness. In a sense, she had made him the excuse to stay in her own limited "safe zone."

The Eagle Awakening was pivotal in so many ways. One fundamental way is that she now has a visceral knowing and memory of what is possible and how she can blend the spiritual path with the human journey of mother and wife. Even more so, she realized these human experiences *were* the fodder for her spiritual journey of Awakening. It was what she had chosen, not just as a human, but also as a soul.

As she pondered these thoughts, she embraced the memory of Shahalaku and the Utopian Land of Waterfalls. She considered the latest development that she was sensing from her soul-kin and how she was Awakening to the erotic fire that activated her desire to explore another way to experience her role as Hōwaka-heh to her community.

She felt the energy of her Spirit Guides gently, yet passionately, whisper in her ear:

"It is time to fully embrace the choices you have made in this life as a reflection of your ReMembering of Oneness — to honor the path of bringing together, in your unique way, the sacred and the human, to embody the beauty of this blending and to recognize the power it holds. You, along with many other way-showers of your time who walk the spiritual path with both human love and Divine Love, lighten the burden of those attempting to be just one or the other. It allows you to be more expansive and to receive support from your beloved whose soul has offered to carry the gift of navigating form as you bring the gift of exploring the formless.

"As you behold the beauty of merging the worlds you inhabit as Beki and Shahala, each equal to the other, your definition of Utopia will expand to include ALL. From this knowing that all is equal and all, at its very essence, IS Love, you will release the impulse to judge yourself or the other. You will truly know the magic of Unconditional Love and the Awakened Consciousness you yearn to embody again. When you release your need to 'other' another in any way, to regulate anyone or anything to the polarized roles of victim, villain, or savior, you will liberate yourself from the suffering you feel and witness amongst the people of your time. You will have more capacity to lean in and feel the heart of another without becoming consumed by what is broken. You will access the infinite resource of healing that embodies a Truth beyond the human mind and the technologies born of this mind—the Truth of Wholeness, Creation, and this Divine Essence within all beings. You will see the journey of each embodied soul as perfect unto itself and not be distracted by the conditions that seem to indicate otherwise.

"It is this frequency that heals you and the apparent 'other.' For in Oneness, there is no 'other,' dear one. As you embrace your Wholeness without concern or attachment to the gaze of another, you will finally feel the true belonging that surpasses understanding and is felt as ecstasy, peace, clarity, knowing, trust, and Divine Wisdom. You will feel the Love that is You! You will never feel alone again."

Beki remembered the invitation of her father's words spoken through Myrna many months earlier: *"Come on in. The water is warm. What are you waiting for?"*

Those bothersome, uninvestigated thoughts and beliefs that, like static in the background, made her afraid of moving into this unchartered territory. She recently heard a profound perspective that helped her to release some of her resistance: "The only thing you will ever find in the Unknown is more of yourself." Of course! Yet, from the human dimension of separation consciousness, it was easy to forget that there is only One of us and that the "scary" world *out there* is essentially a reflection of what was in her own mind and consciousness. It was a strange, ubiquitous, undefined expectation that something "out there" would be less safe and comfortable than the reality she now inhabited. This is why so many people stay stuck or evolve slower than they want to. These unconscious beliefs often override the true and wild desires born through the heart sent as an impulse by their Soul.

Beki simply sat in recognition of this knowing. She wondered what words would emerge on her screen next that would continue to reveal the merging paths of these two parts of her Soul – herself and Shahalaku.

THIRTY-FOUR

Sacred Meeting

Yeshua hua mali mama
Wa'kamema
Wala'koko
Hōli Hōli Hōli
Ha'mana Hōli Haa

Shahalaku peered into the glowing crystal sphere as Haka had instructed her. As she did, she could see a scene unfolding as though it was a holographic movie. Not only could she hear and see the details distinctly, but she could also viscerally feel it at a very deep level. This ritual was not unlike the process she had experienced with Namundhi as the two of them explored Beki's life so that they could determine where to insert their influence for her Awakening. However, since she was the receiver rather than the facilitator of this activation of Wah'halama, it felt more focused and intense. Its purpose was specific to her and this burgeoning desire to open to the Erotic fire within her to magnetize the lover that would be her mate.

At first, she was uncertain what this scene had to do with her intention, although she knew the potency of Haka's medicine and completely trusted the process. She also trusted in her Soul and the creative ways It always brought her into full alignment with her desires.

Within the shimmering crystal, she watched a beautiful young woman with a spirit so powerful she could feel the rays of her light penetrate the time and space between them. Her small, humble dwelling was warm and inviting. She was leaning over her child, who must have been only three years old. He had a head of thick, dark, curly hair that reminded her of the luscious, black locks of Beki's youngest son. His eyes were dark pools of dancing love that looked deeply into his mama's eyes. He reached up to caress her cheek with a smile, and she bent over to kiss him as she tucked him into the bed.

Shahala felt her heart swell with the demonstration of love and tenderness between the two. It was nothing like she had ever witnessed before, even in her world of extraordinary intimacy and Oneness. This was unique and had a profound effect on her heart. She could feel a radiant, warm sensation envelop her whole being. She wondered what was happening. When she thought her heart could not expand anymore, she watched as the woman turned around to walk into the room where a tall man with a full, dark beard and equally curly locks stood waiting for her at the threshold of their bedroom. He took her hand and grinned with a mischievous look of longing. Shahala felt his complete adoration for his wife as much as she could sense the erotic flame between them.

He gently coaxed her into their room and danced with her around the bed before sweetly kissing the back of her neck, pulling her silky, soft, black hair to the side. She laughed with delight. The scent of his skin was a mix of sandalwood with a hint of frankincense. Shahala could smell it and feel the intoxicating energy between them begin to warm and moisten her own loins. The passion they shared matched the love they felt for each other. The mutual respect and care they took as they made love quietly in this modest yet sacred space, adjacent to the room where the little boy slept soundly, was extraordinary. The feelings of both adults were being transmitted to Shahala through this process of the activated Soul Memory of the human collective.

As this erotic, sweet, sensuous scene began to fade, another image emerged within the crystal ball. The man in the last scene was with his son, teaching him how to create a wooden chest ornately carved with butterflies and birds. The little boy must have been closer to nine years old now, and he was eager to take the tools from his father to make this chest all by himself to give as a gift to his mother. His father laughed and patiently allowed him to take the carving tools while he supervised without too much intervention. It was artful to watch how this man offered his assistance while giving the boy the space to find his own unique self-expression.

Then, another scene showed the whole family of five boys with the two parents walking through the town. Shahala sensed the fullness of their lives and the responsibility of raising five sons. At the same time, she could feel the joy and pride that the couple felt as they watched the rambunctious boys tussle with each other on the dusty roads. There was so much laughter it made Shahala giggle aloud. The joy was as palpable as the passion she sensed as she witnessed their embodied expression of love.

Only until the next scene emerged did she understand what this journey was revealing. The woman was weeping uncontrollably, and her husband was holding her as she shook. He was stoic and strong in his emotional countenance, but Shahala could also feel the depth of his heartbreak. Then the image of Yeshua, the man that once was the sweet little boy with wild, black curls, was nailed to a cross; his head limp, his tearful eyes beseeching, his heart wide open, with heaving breath becoming softer, slower, and soon…no more.

Shahala gasped with the ache of the mother's anguish, the weight of the father's grief, and the stillness of the dying Yeshua nailed to the cross. As this beautiful, young, brown man took his last breath, his eyes opened, and a blazing fire of unfathomable love burst forth, bathing the entire space around him with soft light and a tangible vibration like nothing any of those present had ever known before. Shahala witnessed and felt the frequencies splinter out into the entire Universe like a supernova explosion. The crystal sphere shimmered with the light of Love that was not only born from the heart of the beloved Yeshua but originated from the Divine Mother embodied by Mary, sustained by the grounded love of his human father.

Haka artfully waved her hand over the image in the crystal and showed the souls of the three beings embracing within the swirling, magnetizing colors of the space beyond worlds, each a Universe unto itself, dancing and blending with the other in a miraculous expression of Love and Light.

Shahala heaved, drawing in a deep breath. Her golden-green eyes were wet and glistening with awe. When she thought she could bear no more, she felt her chest slowly heating up. She pressed her palm to her heart as the energy and heat engulfed her, and the ache of human love poured into her like a thick liquid. It burned and felt cool all at once. She began to moan and sway, holding her chest, feeling the sweetness and sorrow, the ecstasy and the anguish all at once.

She was given the gift of ReMembering what so many humans have lived through since time immemorial. The heartbreak that tears the heart open is alchemy. The sorrow and anguish are equal to the ecstasy and joy it embodies. When brought together without resistance, without judgment, this human love is a magnificent expression of immeasurable Beauty. Just like in the love between Mother Mary and Yeshua and the erotic love shared between her and her beloved husband, Joseph, it catalyzes a potent gift to the Universe that expands beyond the time-space continuum. Yeshua was the embodiment of Unconditional Love, and he infused this frequency into the human love paradigm on Earth at that time. It was an act of profoundly sacred service with untold layers of wisdom and gifts within his life.

Shahalaku felt herself soften with this awareness, releasing any resistance that she initially sensed from the unexpected intensity of this transmission. As her heart opened even more with this softening and this energetic shift emanating from her own essence, she peered into the crystal that had become infused with a rainbow of brilliant light. Emerging from the crystalline colors was a male face, his eyes sparkling with a knowing smile. It seemed as though he was filled with the Universe, or was he the Universe becoming form? She was mesmerized.

Suddenly, Shahalaku burst into tears. Her heart beat to the rhythm of a tone within the crystal, foreign yet familiar all at once. Recognition followed. Her beloved, born of the stars, reached through time and space and entered her longing-filled heart. Her body received this penetrating Love with undulating shivers of sensual, ecstatic explosions. She heard a voice, deep and soft, enter her mind:

"Shahala, my dear beloved one, we meet again, and we shall offer a new kind of love and light to the world with our shared breath, our grounded love, our commitment to Oneness, and the embodiment of this quenching elixir. We will blend together in form and beyond form and experience the All That Is within our embrace. We will dance on stars and travel to worlds that only the two as One can sense. We will know our humanness and that which knows its unlimitedness all at once. I am here with you now and will embrace your form soon."

Just as Shahala felt these words enter her heart and his glorious face penetrate her soul, Beki sensed a ripple of energy ignite her being. In *her* world and time, the moon was full casting a soft light into her room. Rousing from her sleep, feeling the sumptuous waves of energy tingling through her body, she rolled towards her beloved and put her arms around him, pulling him towards her. His body's warmth was always a surprise, and how their bodies met, with the sensation of erotic energy building between them, never ceased to amaze her. She nestled her head against his back and felt overwhelming gratitude for his presence. Tears rolled down her face as she felt the wide, warm opening of her heart, unknowingly, in concert with her soul-kin across dimensions beyond time and space.

THIRTY-FIVE

☉ne

Haa Whya Whoo
Hōlima Hōlima Hōlima Haa

Beki sensed the potency of the transmission that came through the words she typed into her manuscript. It was no coincidence that it was Easter, the Holiday celebrated by Christians all over the globe to honor the resurrection of Jesus Christ three days after his crucifixion. She realized that as Shahala was being given the awareness of Mother Mary, Yeshua, and Joseph and the dynamics of Divine *and* human love, she *too* was receiving this transmission. Beki felt a loosening of her resistance to the human way of loving. She realized that she was being offered an Awakening through Shahalaku's vision: to recognize the beauty and power of human love as *equal* and kin to the Unconditional Divine Love that she had so exalted. It is not one or the other; rather, it is the unfettered allowing and acceptance of both experiences that brings forth a potent and transformational expression of the Oneness that is ALL.

It was a powerful epiphany for Beki to realize that anytime we resist anything, anyone, or any condition, including the state of attached love common in the human experience, we disconnect ourselves from the "other," creating the experience of separation rather than Oneness. Yet, even this is a gift. Experiencing the many diverse ways to feel polarity and separation offers an opportunity to grow and expand the experience of Oneness. Beki marveled at this great orchestration and dynamic dance of creation.

While the world of Shahalaku expresses the conscious awareness of Oneness in contrast to the world of Beki, which seems so dense and removed from this core knowing, both worlds inform the other on this journey of self-realization and self-expression. If we remember that All are One and the One is All, then the creation of *all* experiences serves the expansion and expression of the Whole.

Beki sensed this revelation sink in. The process of *ReMembering* and *re-Awakening* to this Ultimate Truth is incredibly rich with nuance and the opportunity for deeper understanding. She was intrigued with how the creative meaning-making seemed infinite. As she absorbed this knowing, letting it percolate with a sense of curiosity, she felt the words of her Guides offer some insight:

"You are, my dear one, like the Mother Mary that seeks to embody and express Divine Love. You, too, have chosen to do this as and through the mother archetype. Before incarnating as Beki, you longed to bring this emanation of Divine Love to the world during the time and space you now embody. In your understanding of the dynamic energy of human love as both a mother and a wife, you have defined and grown your awareness of the Unconditional Love that seems so elusive in human consciousness.

"Mary is a beautiful example of a Priestess and Avatar of her time who embodied this blended Love, bringing the Divine and human together through the unique way she loved her beloved and all her sons. During this lifetime and many of her lifetimes, Mary embodied the Divine Feminine and devoted her lives to anchoring this frequency in many timeframes on Earth. She continues to do this from the spirit realm. Bringing forth her son, Yeshua, was a part of this mission. He, along with his beloved, Mary Magdalene, came to Earth to reactivate and anchor the Divine Feminine at a time when the imbalanced energy of patriarchy was wreaking havoc.

It was a radical and bold mission that made human life perilous for them both.

"The subsequent interpretations of their human relationship, which portrayed Magdalene as a whore, disempowered her role as the Priestess she truly was. It also implied that Jesus did not engage in sexual human love, marriage, or fatherhood. With his life story becoming fodder for the largest religion of your current time, a perception of what is Divine and holy as separate from erotic love, so intrinsic to the human experience, prevailed."

Beki resonated with these words as she typed them on her screen. Then she felt a distinct voice emerge from beyond form, who introduced himself as Tuala. He explained that he was there to *"help stitch together the memories and patches of the lives so you can understand the individual experiences."*

She felt his words penetrate her mind: *"Your own experiences in many lives included several times in which you were a Priest/ess solely dedicated to the people, unable to marry or have children, as this was believed to be something that would take away from your duties. There were also several lives where you were a wise woman, a medicine woman, who had a family. It was considered that these relationships made you stronger and more empowered.*

"For the people who gave up the rich connection of family in order to serve in the temple, it was typical that the longing for a partner and children became part of everyday life and made service in the temple burdensome. While many people believed, including in your time, that giving up family is necessary for service, in fact, the person who is settled and happy with family is considered inherently more powerful."

He continued, *"You are stitching together your experiences and weighing within yourself, 'Does one nullify the other? Is one greater than the other? What is the true answer here?'"*

Beki contemplated Tuala's words. She could feel the energy of all these soul-kin/iōwayah'ho-kiki congregating around her with all that they had lived and were now living in this eternal moment. She especially felt the sweet and potent Awakening energy of Shahalaku vibrating through her *own* body. She considered all the other selves that she was unaware of experiencing their own version of dynamically blending their love and service to the Divine with the love and commitment of their human relationships. Tuala had offered a window of perception into the many selves and how they were a part of her Soul Memory. It all felt so much clearer now.

Beki pondered Tuala's question, answering it in her mind: *Both ways had value, and one was not better than the other.* She felt that she was being given an awareness of her personal journey as a multidimensional being. She was grateful to feel the assurance offered by Tuala of the value of having a family within the context of providing the services of healer, Priestess/Hōwaka-heh.

Tuala responded to her thoughts, *"There is value there because the healer does not find herself thinking that she has sacrificed everything in order to help others."* He finished his transmission with these words:

"All selves hold a portion of the truth, and all selves hold one Truth."

Beki felt the power of this statement and yet could not entirely make sense of it in her mind. She felt so full she was overflowing. She could feel the resonance with what she had just received. She also appreciated all she had learned from her most intimate relationships as mother and wife and how they informed so much of her work as a Healer/Guide. Indeed, her journey as a mother was why she was drawn to the energetic healing arts she now practiced. The contractions born of the love for her sons sent her on a quest for healing, expansion, and freedom. As she had forged her path of Awakening through her healing process, she was brought to the very tools she now offers others to support them to *ReMember* and to realize their Wholeness again:

It all is a beautiful and wonderful winding path
back home
to the Oneness
that embodies the All.

Haa Whya Whoo
Haa Whya Whoo
Haa Whya Whoo
Tatata taa!

Beki, Shahalaku, and all the other soul-kin felt the ripple of Love penetrating the illusory space and time between them. In a flash, a moment that stretched into forever within the eternal now, they felt the convergence of their essence. Each embodied soul, distinct divine expressions of the One Soul, stretched their consciousness to feel the Eternal Infinite One that encompassed All. They laughed all at once, feeling the waves of goosebumps ripple across their skin. The hairs on their bodies reached towards their Beloved, making Love with the One.

It was
It is
Ecstasy!

THIRTY-SIX

Balance

Toko-magua Hōlima
Wanahaa takina tatata taa

As the erotic fire grew within Shahalaku, it seemed the energy of passion in Beki had become more focused on her intense desire to serve and support others in healing within the world of deep polarity where many suffered. While Beki was inspired by the ignition of Shahala's Awakened Eros, she also noticed how her own fire had fizzled by the sense of responsibility she bore with the roles she loved so much. Sometimes, the balance was lost, particularly when worry for her loved ones consumed her.

Ever since her mother experienced the heart event several months prior, Beki had noticed her erotic fire dampen. She entered a phase she knew well. It was the ebb of her flow, and when it was prolonged, she would notice that her lover's kiss would feel less sweet while she tended to the responsibilities of her people. She mused at how the heat in her body was plagued more with menopausal hot flashes rather than consumed with the heat of erotic longing. She envied Shahalaku.

One day, after offering an extended healing session with a friend who was entering her "end-of-life" transition, Beki felt her inner scale tip and her balance teeter. While Beki thought she was perfectly fine, she soon began to realize that she was absorbing the symptoms of those close to her who were struggling with physical conditions: Her son was concerned with some irregular and strange heart symptoms and was seeking medical assistance to see what was going on. Her mother continued to feel weak and short of breath. Her husband sustained a back injury, which was causing him considerable pain and immobility. Another son was dealing with a toothache, while the youngest son was having a meltdown from the stress of end-of-year exams. It was an avalanche of conditions — a perfect storm for Beki to take on the stress of others and feel it reflected in her own body.

Beki remembered when she was in a session with Myrna, and one of her Life Guides, Ama, offered an insight that made more sense now than ever. She said, *"There is a quality of those who practice the healing arts to take on something of the level of hurt or disability that mirrors that of others around them. This may be conscious or not. There needs to be a conscious push in a continual way to affirm health and prosperity in all areas."*

When depleted, Beki was more likely to take on the energies affecting others — her family and clients. The guidance she received from Spirit focused on the need to be consistent with her rituals to strengthen personal boundaries by clearing energies that did not belong to her and chanting prayers to affirm her Wholeness. These were things that Beki would sometimes forget to do until she noticed herself slipping into this tendency to absorb the physical or emotional symptoms of others, especially with her family. Her Guides were also emphatic about her need to restore, rest, and even occasionally take a sabbatical from the work.

Namundhi's familiar voice came through Myrna with clarity, sharing her wisdom and concern: *"Hello, my sister, my flesh and bone, my friend of the soul. We have witnessed your frustration, and we are cognizant of the demands upon you. In this space, it is necessary to work from the outside in, to eat nourishing food, to drink restorative water, and to sleep, rest, and breathe. You must say: 'That is all I am prepared to do.' The ancient practice of a routine day of observance is very effective – when nothing except essential communication occurs, where one does not offer up service but instead is open to receive service, where one simply sits and basks in the Divine and the mysteries of nature. In the same way that you draw on the gifts of the Earth to nurture others, you must allow yourself to let the Earth nourish you. Take one day out of every seven without feeling you are being called back to work, no work planned, not even picking up a piece of clothing."*

Namundhi recognized that while Shahala was experiencing the burgeoning flame of erotic desire for the first time, to maintain this fire and stay in balance with the confluence of sexual passion with the passion of selfless service it would require intention and practice. As she witnessed the challenges that Beki experienced throughout her life in creating balance with her many nurturing roles, she could see how Shahala, too, would need to draw on new skills to maintain balance. This would also offer an example to other Hōwaka who may choose the path of romantic partnership and perhaps a family. The role of the caretaker takes many forms, and there is a particular quality of empathy one often possesses when drawn to this service. When out of balance, this empathetic nature can become a less healthy expression when the giver has forgotten how to receive, restore, and be filled.

As Beki contemplated the lack of fire she was feeling, she acknowledged how her mother's health condition had initiated this shift. The feeling of worry and responsibility took over and sucked all the sexy out of her. This is the challenge many mothers and caretakers encounter in attempting to maintain the erotic flame with their partner or within themselves. Yet, it is critical for sustaining a healthy relationship and nourishing the whole self. Beki knew that the potency of Eros and the passion it inspires is an empowering resource that she is able to alchemize in all she creates and offers in service.

Now that Beki's children were all young men, she had been looking forward to this intimate time with her husband unhindered by the intense focus on their sons and their needs. Of course, the quest for balance had been ongoing since their sons were very young. Beki was grateful how she and her beloved had managed to maintain a strong sexual attraction toward each other as their love deepened and matured over time. Yet, as many people realize, as their children need them less, the focus is often redirected to caring for aging parents in some way or another. In Beki's case, her vocation as a healer blossomed as her children got older, allowing her the energy to redirect her nurturing nature toward service to the spiritual and emotional well-being of others in her practice. The need for intentional balance was essential.

Beki took to heart the suggestions of her Spirit Guides and particularly loved the advice offered by her beloved Namundhi, whose friendship traversed time and space as she shared her love and insights with Beki *and* Shahala, each an aspect of her Eternal Self. What an amazing communion. Beki felt her heart melt with gratitude. She began to consider which day of the week she might assign as her *"day of observance."* She sensed that if she could be more intentional about restoring her energy, not only would she be less likely to mirror the symptoms of others, but she would begin to feel her erotic flame grow and flow again.

In her next session with Myrna, she received a powerful, uncompromising message from several of her Spirit Guides, including Namundhi. The first Guide that showed up was new. He revealed himself as Pathool and responded to Beki's inquiry about what she most needed to hear, understand, and remember now.

He answered with clarity: *"To remain in balance as you are out in the world, and to seek restoration of balance when you have retreated from it."*

Myrna said he was holding an old-fashioned brass scale in one hand and a flowering rod in the other with white blooms and a yellow center. He also had a golden vessel filled with cool water. He had markings on his face — an upside-down triangle on his forehead, a right-side-up triangle on his chin, and an arrow on each cheek.

He continued, *"There must be a balance between the feminine and masculine energies. There must be a correct meeting of the balance between worldly and spiritual energies. And there must be a correct blending between the work and restorative energies. When all energies are balanced, the rod blooms."*

174

Beki could see the obvious theme Pathool was imparting. It was punctuating, in a new way, the need for restoration and balance that Namundhi had clarified in her last communication with her.

Pathool took it further, *"The end always leads back to the beginning. The beginning is Eden. We are all searching for Eden. You are looking to bring Eden into the work and into the self, and the blooming of the rod means you have completed your portion of the work. There must be a blessing for you, not just for those who are coming to you for the blessing.*

"You are the rod. If you are in bloom, balance is achieved. If not in bloom, balance needs to be restored. You are one of the branches of the Tree of Life, and the Earth is waiting for your season of blooming."

Beki breathed in the poetry of his words as they went directly into her soul. In that moment it was easy for her to understand the meaning of this metaphor encompassing the biblical archetype of the Utopia of Eden, the primordial essence of true balance. As she wrote about the Land of Waterfalls, the Utopian world of Hōlawai'kiki, it felt like her own personal Eden. For Beki, writing about this journey with Shahalaku has returned her to this primal Garden of Eden, the original home of her human soul. At the same time, it has been a way for her to bring Eden to the here and now of her current time and space.

When Beki asked about the erotic fire that seemed to have dwindled, Pathool continued with this theme of balance, which Beki recognized as an essential foundation for life. It made her think of how the "story of separation" could also be considered a story of extreme imbalance. To embrace Oneness was not to be the *same* as the other, but to fully embrace each being in their unique, distinct expression of the Infinite One.

"The male essence and female essence are out of balance," Pathool said. *"There is a desire to nurture which is in opposition to the desire to ravage. When one is in the role of parent or child, the passionate nature routes itself to other things. The man does not wish to ravage his mother, and the mother does not wish to ravage her son."*

Beki contemplated these words and could see how the mother's role could take precedence when she felt worried and burdened by the caretaker's responsibility. This certainly reflected her moving out of balance. How interesting to see these nuances and how they affected her feelings of intimacy, arousal, and connection with her spouse. It was not the outer conditions that caused this imbalance necessarily. It was the way she *dealt* with the conditions. Beki felt excited by these revelations, for they chipped away at her old story that impacted all areas of her life.

Pathool continued, "*The roles are out of position and must be restored with a simple touch, emotional connection, and a reaffirmation, as one examines the spectrum of true commitment and partnership brought back into its proper sphere and given the motivation of life-giving — each taking and each giving in equal measure.*"

The transmission from Pathool was complete. Beki marveled at his insistence on firmly anchoring this message of Balance. She wondered what her other Guides might offer to enhance her understanding of herself and the evolution of her Being.

THIRTY–SEVEN

Fire and Water

Tani koma wa'haa
Ayowey heh'nee
Takina holi'whya ha iōwai nanee

Ayowey, the Angel of Healing, piped in with her own transmission of wisdom and compassion. *"A large part of the artistic mindset, a large part of the healer-role, is in receiving the same degree of passion that is given out in art or in the offering up of the sacrifice for healing. Both impulses are built on fire, and so is the natural human sexual element. The fire (in you) is out. It has been doused with the water that surrounds you. You must move to higher ground, further up the mountain, where there is no damp Earth or wet leaves to hinder or impede your progress. You must seek each other in a way that affirms the very beginning of life, the very origins of the cosmos. It is this impulse that will create a new spark —a spark that has not gone away but has dampened and is creating smoke around you. Seek higher ground. Do not be afraid of the fire. It is the element that has given birth to you.*

"Sexual congress is our gift to you."

Beki looked puzzled by this terminology and asked what she meant by "congress."

Ayowey replied, *"A meeting of physical bodies as a conduit for the meeting of souls."*

"Who is offering this gift?" Beki asked.

"Those of us who live in paradise," she answered.

Beki felt a sense of awe. She immediately thought of the last time she was *literally* in the mountains with her beloved, less than a year ago, where her erotic fire was raging. It inspired him to ravage her, matching her passion with his. It was an extraordinary time of reigniting the flame of their erotic love at a time when all their children were forging their own paths of independence. Indeed, the metaphor of the mountain was apt.

Namundhi was eager to interject. She had been present all along, excited by what was being offered, and had been a part of orchestrating this important discourse. She knew that not only would Beki benefit from these insights, but also those who would read the book would recognize themselves in this scenario of the dampening fire and receive guidance from this transmission from Spirit. Of course, Namundhi's primary intention was to support both Beki and Shahala in their evolution.

"Let me tell you what your dilemma is." She spoke with authority.

"One must not create what one is. One must create the opposite of yourself. If you are in water, how can you create water? When you are living in water, there is no inspiration to create more. If you are on fire, if you are thirsty, if you are sweating, all you can think about is water. There is the necessary feeling of necessity, the understanding of what is opposite, to bring interest, inspiration and motivation, to create."

There was that familiar idea of contrast and polarity as a potent quality necessary for growth, expansion, evolution, and even inspiration. Beki had written about this in her book *Bare Beauty: My Journey of Awakening,* in which she described the many life "contractions" that gave rise to expansion and inspiration. Often, these challenging experiences would serve as a catalyst to give birth to the desire for transformation. Namundhi's poetic metaphor resonated with this inner knowing.

She continued, *"As long as you dwell inside the water, like a mermaid, you will never create water that sparks your interest. You must climb the volcano, walk on hot lava, and feel the intense heat of the storm that has nothing to do with water until you can see water in its life-giving form. This is not saying, 'I have no interest.' This says, 'I am a citizen of the ocean, and I am only dreaming of seeing what dry land looks like.' You come from fire."*

Beki was mesmerized by the lyrical sounds of dancing words that painted pictures and sought to penetrate her weary soul, reminding her of the truth of her nature. Her words called her back home to the fire that she would douse with the water that *also* nourished her. This balance seemed so elusive at times. When she floated *too* long in the gentle ocean waves, she would feel lulled to sleep and risk drowning.

Beki explored these thoughts with Myrna. She shared that she and her partner were both water signs in the zodiac. She was a Scorpio, and he was a Pisces. She wondered about this idea of her *"coming from fire,"* a theme that kept showing up throughout this transmission. When she asked for more clarity about this, Myrna asked her who she wanted to talk to. Beki sensed that Namundhi had more to say and said so.

"My sister, you come to the right source for information." Myrna smiled big as she translated Namundhi's words and Soul essence. Beki could feel the love and kinship between them as she continued to offer guidance.

"You originate typically in areas that are warmer than average. You seek the sun. You do not enjoy your lives on snowy mountains, ice flows, or areas where there is more dark than light. You seek sunrise, not the sunset. You are looking for hot sand between your toes. It is only in appreciation of how much heat is around you that you understand the pleasures of moving into the water, feeling the quenching of your spirit, and knowing that water meets fire and creates steam that rises to the heavens. You may be a sign that seeks water, but you seek water not because you are a drop of the ocean but because you are the red-orange flame that comes from the source of fire. You are seeking the coolness, the quenching activity of the water, and you are looking forward to the steam — the way steam hydrates

179

and the way that it moves. It is a powerful force that can only be realized by the meeting of fire and water."

Of course, Beki resonated with these words. While her early life was spent in Canada with long, cold winters, it was when she moved to a tropical island in the Bahamas that she felt at home. It was where her art flourished, and her body and soul Awakened to the heat of passion. After her high school years in Nassau, she returned to Canada for University and later to Boston, where the cold climate was unbearable for her fiery nature. She eagerly moved south to Charleston, South Carolina, where Sherman was stationed after enlisting in the Air Force.

Namundhi continued giving her insight into who she was, not just in this life as Beki, but as the Soul Essence that traversed many of her embodied lives. She was intrigued. Beki asked her, "What is the best way to reignite this fire within my relationship?"

"You are the fire. You burn to the touch.
You are not afraid of water even though it can squelch you.
You consume.
Your energy towards your water friend must be one of intense heat.
It must be consuming energy.
You must tell him,
'Focus on me and only me.
See the red and the orange of my flame, and when you do,
if you are privileged, you will see the blue
of energy that is being consumed,
the oxygen,
the single most needed material in the world to sustain life.'
It is in the blue,
that is at the very center of that flame,
that must be met with the blue
which is the very molecule of the water that creates life.
This is true balance.
He must be consumed by you.
He must seek to quench the fire you offer."

Wisely, Beki asked for a point of focus, a mantra, a practice, to align her with this inner fire element. She could not get enough of the gift of this communion with her soul sister from another life.

"The rising sun is your point of focus.
How it sets fire to the night sky
How it lights up the entire Earth
How it makes plants grow
How it turns water into steam
How it inspires others to see color and beauty
How it infuses the rainbows
which is a water sign itself
Your mantra shall be:
'As the sun rises every day,
so do I.
As the phoenix burns and is consumed by the fire
and is resuscitated by its own ashes,
I, too, do not fear consumption by fire.
I live for it.
And in offering the intense heat that flows through me
and outwardly into the Earth,
I help others burn away what is no longer needed
and with the person who is my other,
with the person who has contracted
to offer love and support to me,
I offer the gift of consumption
and I receive the gift of dwelling."

Deep breath…

Beki and Myrna were both speechless. Beki *breathed* in the mantra, feeling its potency, the deep resonance, and ReMembering. *"Dwelling,"* she repeated, with a sigh, feeling the vastness of this precious gift her beloved offered her that gave her a sense of home, of belonging, providing for her the ground to land on after a long flight into the world beyond form. He was the water that quenched her heat when her passion sought release. He was the West to her East. Indeed, he was the yang to her yin. He was the gardener who tended to the Eden, the lush, sacred sanctuary that fed her soul.

She was overwhelmed with gratitude and expressed her appreciation to Namundhi for her gift of this sharing. Namundhi's response brought tears to Beki's eyes. *"These words you gave me some time ago. You are the author. You are the originator of these thoughts. I simply offer them back to you in your time of wondering."*

Thirty-Eight

Conclusion

Beki marveled at the lush beauty of the efflorescing, verdant forest enveloping the winding path where she walked briskly on this crisp, cool afternoon. The sun was shining after two days of gray skies, an anomaly in the subtropical climate of her home near the sea. She loved the large oak trees with inviting, strong limbs that begged to be climbed. The Spanish moss swayed in the breeze; pollen covered the path. Palm trees of all kinds found their place among the tall pines and ancient oaks. Occasionally, Beki would be pleasantly accosted by the sweet scent of honeysuckle, and she would pause to relish the intoxicating aroma with deeper breaths. She thought about how the blooms of these trees and plants were offering healing frequencies that she would, in turn, offer her clients in a bottle in the form of flower essences: pine for self-compassion, oak for restoring energy and balance when overworked, and honeysuckle for grief and releasing the past. Just like the world of her soul-kin, nature provides all we need to thrive.

Beki's mind was filled with the rhythmical words of her native tongue from another time. She quietly chanted aloud to the cadence of her gait with a sweet melody filling the air mingling with the sounds of the wildlife around her. She smiled as she felt the integration of these worlds, the selves, as the Soul-knowing settled into her being.

"Awella'hah
Awella'ho
Shahalaku
Shahai'kiki

Weeshah'aneylo
Ha'mana Ha Haa

I am that I am
The Loving Self
Holder of Wisdom
Meeting the Truth

I speak the language
of Wholeness and Creation
born of the Sacred Breath"

Beki felt the power and beauty of this sacred soul language and marveled at the journey it had taken her on, assimilating the healing frequencies it embodied into her world and her hamanaku. She now was able to bring a piece of this inner and ancient Utopia back into *this* now, infusing her world with the possibility and blessings it carried.

As she approached her favorite swing to perch on, she looked out at the green expanse of marsh. Instead of the salty scent of the sea air, she drew in a deep breath of the aroma of hyssop. She closed her eyes, lifting her head to the sun, feeling its bright rays meet the heat of her inner fire. In a flash of heart-opening majesty, she saw a purple field of blooming hyssop lining a mountainside stretching as far as her eyes could see. In the middle of the field, she witnessed a beautiful couple, arms outstretched toward each other with hands clasped. Shahalaku and her beloved laughed boisterously. Her thick mane of hair, wild and free, glowed like fire in the raking light as the sun rose. She placed her other hand onto her swollen belly with delight as she felt the movement of the moon, the stars, and the sun dance with zeal in the sacred space within her eternal womb.

Beki felt herself quiver with delight as the ecstasy and joy of Shahala entered her heart. Her mind floated to earlier that morning when her beloved ravished her with his passionate embrace and penetrating love quenching her fire. She smiled at how the advice of her Guides helped her to remember her wild and fiery nature, her inner heat, and the importance of balance and restoration. She marveled at how, without fail, when her state of being and mind shifted *inside* of her, the outer world she perceived quickly reflected that shift. After thirty-seven years of marriage, she certainly had enough experience to see this happen time and time again. She was always grateful to receive deeper insight into the nature of herself, on life, and love. The journey was never ending and her desire to expand was insatiable.

Beki felt a fullness of appreciation for all life's twists and turns — for the magical and the mundane, for the ups and the downs, for the undulating contractions and the ecstatic expansions, for the fiery passion and the watery calm... All of it made her puzzle more whole, more colorful, more textured, and rich.

Yes, it has been a wild and sweet ride, and it has only just begun!

Namundhi whispered a special prayer into Beki's ear in honor of the resurrection of her native tongue:

*"**Mah'aka ano**: A place where there is no time*
***La'esh nay'aneyo**: Those who will hear me please listen*
***Aka waylee ushna'hah**: I humbly beseech you to hear the prayer from my lips*
***Hōla ah'awaylo**: I ask for the peace of your being to dwell inside us*
***Lo'me nee'hah**: As I ask may it be so."*

"Such a lovely language." Beki thought as she sighed with reverence.

"It is pure," Namundhi responded, reading her mind. *"It is the language of Wholeness, the language of Priests, a language of a soul that has not been torn in two."*

EPILOGUE

Beki Speaks

As I sit and contemplate the unfolding of this book, the ReMembering of my parallel self in an alternate dimension as Shahalaku, I am full of appreciation for the journey. I feel a sense of awe at the way my Eternal Soul provides the most creative ways to offer me what I deeply desire. Not only did I receive the experience of a beautiful depiction of Oneness and the personal Utopia that it represents to me, but I also gained a deeper appreciation for how the story of separation serves this desire. As the plot revealed itself to me, I was amazed at how the journey within *my* dimension, which sometimes feels like a dystopia, informed Shahalaku, giving rise to a deep yearning within her that alters and evolves *her* world. This was truly an unexpected twist for me. The potential for evolution is unending.

This story allows me to embody the more complex definition of Oneness and the Unconditional nature of Love that is at Its very essence. For without the story of separation, there is no lived experience of Oneness. Without the in-breath, there is no exhalation. Without the contrasting darkness, how can the light be experienced? Without the dystopian realities, how does one genuinely know the Utopia that they inhabit as Utopian?

Oneness must not be mistaken for sameness. In actuality, it is the opposite. Oneness acknowledges the infinite uniqueness of all its parts, celebrating the intrinsic diversity of All that Is, knowing that it's all a part of the Whole. It seeks not to homogenize the individual expressions of the One but to experience the infinite possibilities embodied by Its parts.

To ReMember our essential nature is to remember that we are all One while simultaneously experiencing the uniqueness of the individual self. This is the Utopia that Shahalaku Awakens in me; that already is within me now. While my soul chooses to explore this theme of Oneness, it does not mean it is the only or best path to realize the True Self. We all come to Earth with unique themes and interests that propel our journey forward. At a Soul level, some of us courageously choose more intense and challenging themes than others to generate the experiences and expansion desired by our Divine Self.

When perceiving from my Soul Self, I more easily see through the lens of Oneness Consciousness, allowing me to appreciate and revel in the Beauty of *all* choices; I am fascinated by the infinite topics of exploration, and I do not judge myself or others for our choices. However, when I am drawn into my drama and get lost in the "dystopian" storylines, it can be more challenging to appreciate the Whole. Yet, this challenge serves its own brilliant purpose. It is necessary to *believe* in the story/drama so that it feels *real*, allowing us to fully experience the wild and wondrous journey we call life on Earth. It offers us the most profound platform for growth and "Soulvolution" to forget our True Self so we can take this brave and creative pilgrimage of ReMembering to return Home once again.

Weeshah'aneylo

*The Language of Wholeness and Creation
and the Sacred Breath*

The ReMembering of this Soul Language has evolved and become more integrated within me, threading the Soul together and connecting me to a time and space in which I am aligned to Oneness. It is genuinely accelerating my embodiment of Oneness. I feel more illuminated by how I operate from the dying paradigm of separation consciousness. This allows me to shift more and more quickly into a state of being and mind that reflects the Truth of Oneness.

I offer these Light Language transmissions during my Soul Sessions with clients so they, too, may receive the potent healing energies by activating the essence of the language: Wholeness and Creation. Like all "Light Languages," it comes through all dimensions to bring what is needed at the moment. It surpasses the linear mind and enters the person at the cellular DNA level, initiating their Inner Knowing and ReMembering.

Now, the sounds and words feel organically natural as they flow from my lips. Yet, in the beginning, I would feel out of breath because of the breathy nature of the language, not to mention my initial challenges adjusting to the new frequencies. It is like acclimating to a new atmospheric altitude. Sometimes, the words flow out, and I have a sense of the meaning. Other times, I receive a direct translation, usually when the recipient would benefit from understanding the meaning, particularly in the case of a Soul Mantra. Yet, there are also times when I have no idea of the meaning, feeling the ripples of energy waft through me with a sense of deep knowing, expansiveness, and reverence. The essence of gratitude is sprinkled through all the words. "*Ta ta taa*" often emerges within the sounds, which I understand as an expression of gratitude and reverence. I have done my best to spell each word phonetically to portray what I hear in my mind and as I speak it aloud. The language has a rhythm and cadence that sometimes feels like a chant or song.

I have noticed over time how every sound/word ends in an out-breath, which Namundhi explained to me in our first meeting during my session with Myrna. She said that each word in the Soul Mantra would contain a numeric value that was indivisible (whole). *"It is the language of Wholeness and Creation, always with the Divine Breath out,"* she shared. This confused me initially because, before I allowed myself to ReMember the language, I could not seem to create a mantra using English using all words ending in the out-breath. Now I understand that it is the language of Weeshah'aneylo that contains only Whole words. My English renditions of the poems/mantras were interpretations of the transmissions from my "native tongue."

In another exchange with my Spirit Guide, Ama, I was offered more insights into this new and ancient language. *"When you first learn a language, you learn the mechanics of it, but when you begin to feel its rhythm and electricity, you no longer need to count your steps. You need to feel the sway, to feel the emotions behind the words, and the words will end up with their own healing potion. You do not need to interfere with that. The idea of the word poem (soul mantra) is that the listener receives it. How you deliver it is up to you. It is impactful because the words themselves offer the opportunity for health and healing."*

In response to my question about the translation that I sometimes receive in English, Ama explained, *"The interpretation lies in the heart, not the brain. It is accompanied and brought into the world through emotion. You are ReMembering the language, but you are accessing the emotion, and of course, you would have equal access to convey this emotion in the language you now speak (English)."*

As someone who speaks only English, I find it fascinating to feel and hear these sounds emerge from my own voice. It feels both strange and completely natural. This book has been a brilliant way to honor the language and allow me to fully embrace this gift to share as an offering of Love, Oneness, and Wholeness.

With Sacred Breath, I speak.
~Beki

GLOSSARY

Akashic Records

- *A **vibrational record** of the Soul's journey through all time and space which contains all memories, feelings, actions, and thoughts.*

Aweesha

- ***Free Will**: The inherent ability to make choices that are not predetermined by past events, highlighting the autonomy and freedom of an individual's soul in the journey of life and spiritual evolution.*

Doosh'dahah Aho

- ***Awaken Now**: A call to immediate Awakening and recognition of one's true nature and connection to the Divine. It emphasizes the urgency and importance of spiritual Awakening in the present moment (Hah'laqua).*

Haa / Ha'mana

- ***Sacred Breath / Love**: Considered synonymous in the language of the Hōlawai, the breath is viewed not merely as a physical necessity but as a sacred act that connects individuals to the Divine essence of creation. It symbolizes the continuous exchange of life force between the self and the cosmos, emphasizing the spiritual significance of breath in sustaining life and spiritual connection.*

Haa Whya Whoo

- **The Divine, Source Energy, God, Infinite One**: Terms used interchangeably to denote the ultimate Source of all creation and existence, embodying the concepts of Divine Presence, Infinite Consciousness, and Universal Energy.

Hah'laqua

- **Eternal Moment of Now**: The present moment, viewed as the only true point of power, existence, and action. It emphasizes the importance of living fully and consciously in the immediate experience, transcending past and future constructs.

Hakamani / Haka

- **Matchmaker**: A role or function within the community dedicated to facilitating connections and relationships that are harmonious and aligned with individual soul paths and purposes.

Hamanaku

- **Exchange of Energy, Gift, Vocation, Purpose, Dharma**: Refers to the unique contribution each individual brings to the world, serving as their spiritual calling. It highlights the interplay of giving and receiving energy in fulfilling one's purpose.

Ha'wahakakaya

- **Pure Love within the Infinite Realm**: Describes the highest and most unconditional form of Love, emanating from and connecting to the Infinite Source. It represents the essence of Divine Love that pervades all existence.

He'kinika-hee

- **Energy**: The fundamental force that animates life and sustains all forms of existence. It underscores the concept that everything is energy, manifesting in various forms and frequencies.

Hōlamakini

- **Sacred sexual union**: *A deeply spiritual act that embodies the physical, emotional, and energetic merging of two beings, celebrated as a powerful expression of love and creation. .*

Hōlawai

- **The people from Hōlawai-kiki**: *Denotes the inhabitants of Hōlawai-kiki, recognized for their deep spiritual understanding and connection to the principles of Oneness and multidimensional consciousness.*

Hōlawai-kiki

- **Land of Waterfalls / Sacred waters to which we Belong**: *A realm characterized by its connection to nature, spirituality, and the harmonious way of life of its inhabitants.*

Hōlimama-Fafui

- **Creation Ceremony**: *A collective spiritual practice aimed at manifesting communal intentions and visions into reality.*

Hōwaka-heh / Hōwaka

- **Priest/ess, Holy Person**: *Spiritual leaders and guides within the community, tasked with facilitating ceremonies, rituals, and the spiritual growth of the inhabitants, serving as intermediaries between the physical and spiritual realms.*

Iōwai

- **Water**: *Symbolizes life, purity, and flow. It is considered a sacred element that sustains life.*

Iōwayah'ho

- **Soul**: *The eternal and Divine essence of an individual, transcending physical existence and connecting each being to the universal Source. It encompasses the totality of one's spiritual journey across lifetimes.*

Iōwayah'ho-kiki

- ***Soul-Kin from an alternate Life/a parallel self***: *Refers to other incarnations or aspects of one's multidimensional Self, acknowledging the connection and kinship between different expressions of the same Soul across various realities.*

Japa

- ***A spiritual practice involving the repetitive chanting or recitation*** *of a mantra or Divine name. Japa is often performed as a form of meditation and devotion, aimed at focusing the mind, deepening spiritual awareness, and connecting with the Divine. It can be done silently, softly, or aloud, and is considered a powerful tool for spiritual growth and inner peace.*

Life Spirit Guides

- ***Non-physical entities that provide guidance, support, and wisdom:*** *Often considered guardians or mentors, they assist individuals on their spiritual journeys.*

Oneness

- ***The fundamental concept that all existence is interconnected:*** *transcending the illusion of separation. Oneness suggests that at the deepest level, every form of life is part of a unified Whole, sharing a common essence with the Source of all creation*

OverSoul

- ***A term used to describe a higher aspect of the embodied soul*** *that oversees and connects the experiences of an individual's various incarnations. It is akin to a collective consciousness that encompasses all the individual soul's embodied experiences across time and space.*

Multidimensional Self

- ***The belief that the self exists not just in the physical realm*** *but across multiple dimensions or planes of existence simultaneously. This concept implies that individuals have aspects of themselves living and experiencing life in different realities or dimensions beyond the physical.*

ReMembering

- *A spiritual process of reconnecting and reintegrating with the universal Whole, transcending beyond mere recollection of past events. It involves Awakening to the inherent unity and interconnectedness of all life.*

Shahalaku

- *The Loving Self: A name chosen to embody the essence of Unconditional Love, wisdom, and the understanding of one's true nature.*

Reiki

- *A form of energy healing involves channeling universal life force energy to promote healing, relaxation, and balance.*

Soul Path Guide

- *A specific type of Spirit Guide focused on an individual's soul journey: offering specialized insight to support the fruition of a particular soul purpose being explored in this lifetime.*

Tah'nani-kiki

- *Animal-kin: Animals or creatures considered part of one's extended family or soul group, recognizing the spiritual connection and mutual respect between humans and all forms of life.*

Toka-Maya

- *Collective Vision: The shared dream or aspiration of a community, envisioned collectively to guide communal efforts towards a common goal or reality, reflecting the power of unified intention.*

Toko-magua

- *Focused attention: The concentrated energy directed towards a specific intention or task. It underscores the importance of mindfulness and intentionality in manifesting outcomes and engaging with the world.*

(Divine) Transmission

- *Communication or insight received directly from a higher spiritual Source or dimension. This encompasses messages, wisdom, and guidance channeled through the Soul, intended to elevate understanding and consciousness.*

Wa'kamema / Mema

- **Mother**: *Emphasizes the role of the mother not only in the biological sense but also as a nurturer and guide within the spiritual and emotional development of the individual and community.*

Wala'koko / Koko

- **Father**: *Highlights the father's role in providing support, guidance, and protection, contributing to the physical, spiritual, and emotional well-being of the family and community.*

Wanahaa

- **Love of Beauty**: *The appreciation and reverence for Beauty in all its forms, recognizing Beauty as a manifestation of the Divine and as an essential aspect of spiritual and Earthly existence.*

Wah'halama

- **Soul Memory**: *The accumulation of knowledge, experiences, and wisdom stored within the Soul, spanning across various lifetimes and dimensions, guiding individuals toward realization and fulfillment.*

Wa'keeda

- **Parent of All**: *Symbolizes the collective responsibility and care shared by the community for the upbringing and well-being of each individual, reflecting a communal approach to nurturing and growth.*

Weeshah'aneylo

- **Language of the Sacred Breath, Wholeness, and Creation**: *A mode of communication that transcends words, embodying the vibrational essence of creation, unity, and the sacredness of existence.*

Xanlahmundhi

- **Namundhi's actual spelling**: *The phonetic simplification for ease of understanding is used in the book, representing a character who embodies wisdom, guidance, and spiritual mentorship within the narrative.*

ACKNOWLEDGMENTS

This book is truly co-authored by Spirit expressed in the voices of my Guides that come through the Akashic Records in my daily meditations along with those channeled through Myrna: Namundhi, Ama, Pathool, Ayowey. I am grateful to them all for their collaboration and especially to my Eternal Soul that connected me to my iōwayah'ho-kiki, Shahalaku, which inhabits the mystical Land of Waterfalls in a parallel dimension. Such a sweet gift!

My deepest gratitude to my Earthly spiritual guides, Chyrs and Myrna who have grounded my connection to the Divine in a tangible, luscious, creative dance. My sessions with Myrna and the Guides, who have come through her, have been the inspiration for this book. The continued support from Chrys offers a way to integrate and embody what Spirit offers.

My heart is full of gratitude for my mother, Elayna, and her unique ability to understand the language of my soul, which has now taken a new form. Just as in my first book, *Bare Beauty*, I was able to share my chapters with her to read and to hold, with reverence, the power and energy of this transmission while it was unfolding. I knew I could trust her to say just enough to add fuel to my creative flame, and not too much, that it could risk derailing the tender process of creation. Not to mention, the portrait of me on the back cover was painted by my mother. I do not take for granted the extraordinary nature of our relationship.

My gratitude extends to Shanen for her generous help in the tedious work of editing; Tamra for her expertise and patience in creating the cover design; My son, Kai, for helping with the layout design; and Banner for the beautiful photos she took of me and my art.

Finally, I am forever grateful for my husband, Sherman, and his willingness to always support me with any technical needs along the way. Mostly his presence and love sustain me and feed me in so many ways. I am blessed beyond dimensions!

ABOUT THE AUTHOR

Beki Crowell

is a Soul Artist and Vibrational Healer, whose creative journey is deeply intertwined with her spiritual practice. Guided by divine inspiration through the wisdom of the Akashic Records, she offers the healing frequencies of Flower Essences, Reiki, and Light Language in her transformative Soul sessions. Through her art, Beki transcends the physical realm, infusing her paintings with divine transmissions that resonate with the frequencies of Beauty, Wholeness, and Oneness.

Particularly remarkable are her Soul portraits, where she channels your Soul onto canvas, revealing your Inner Being who is innately whole, powerful, and free. Each painting holds sacred codes of the Divine Self, offering timely activations for the Awakening process.

Beki's first memoir, *Bare Beauty: My Journey of Awakening*, mirrors her spiritual evolution and serves as a testament to her unwavering commitment to personal growth and enlightenment. With the release of her second memoir, *Threading of the Soul: ReMemberng Oneness and the Multidimensional Self*, Beki continues to activate frequencies of Love, Creation, and Divine Wisdom, contributing to the collective ReMembering and the emergence of a New Earth. **www.bekiart.com**

From the Beauty and breadth at the edge of the sea
I feel the stirring of a new and ancient chant
blending the heart of the Universe
with the mind of those
walking the journey on Earth.

Om Namah Shahala
Om Namah Shahala
Om Namah Shahala
Om Namah
Shahalaku

In reverence and awe, I bow to the Loving Self

Made in United States
Orlando, FL
26 September 2024

51954789R00124